BEFORE THE LIGHT

SAMANTHA HICKS

ALSO BY SAMANTHA HICKS

Trusting Hearts
After the Dark
Unknown Forces

BEFORE THE LIGHT

SAMANTHA HICKS

Albrity
Rainbow Publications

2020

Before the Light
© 2020 by Samantha Hicks

Affinity E-Book Press NZ LTD
Canterbury, New Zealand

1st Edition

ISBN: 978-1-98-858841-4

Editor: CK King
Proof Editor: Alexis Smith
Cover Design: Irish Dragon Design
Production Design: Affinity Publication Services

ACKNOWLEDGMENTS

The past couple of years have been the best of my life. I never thought I would be a published author and be part of such a wonderful community. None of it would have been possible without the great people at Affinity. They make the publishing process easy and trouble free. I am always amazed at how well they improve my writing and guide me in the right direction. Thank you for continuing to work with me and take chances on my books.

Nancy has designed another amazing cover—one I'm a little in love with—and I admire her artistic eye.

CK did a brilliant job in editing. I learned so much about sentence structure and flow from this process that will no doubt make the next book even better.

It takes a lot of people to bring this novel to you, the reader, in its best possible shape, and I'm forever thankful to be working with this group of ladies. Here's to many more projects in the future.

Obviously, I need to thank my family and friends for their continued support, and a special mention to Finley, my springer spaniel. Writing full time is a lonely process, but his companionship makes my day a lot less boring—constantly cleaning up after him and playing never fails to fill my day when I'm not sat at my desk.

And last but not least, thank you to the readers who enjoy my work and take the time to reach out and connect, leave a review, or even a mention on social media. Without your support and encouragement, I wouldn't be able to do the thing I love most, creating characters that will hopefully stay with you long after the last page has been read.

DEDICATION

For Gladys and Ralph Warren,
the most amazing grandparents in the world.
Forever in my heart.

TABLE OF CONTENTS

PROLOGUE

June 2018

Kathleen Bowden-Scott sat in Dmitry's wine bar, nursing her second glass of champagne. Rebecca sat across from her. They'd met a few days ago. Kathleen had ignored Rebecca's text message, late Friday night, asking to meet up again for drinks, but Saturday morning she decided she needed the distraction. She lied to Meredith. Kathleen racked her brain trying to figure out if this was the first time she had ever lied to Meredith. It was. She told Meredith she would be working away. Instead, she was here having drinks with another woman.

"Somebody finally decided to meet with me," Rebecca teased. She tilted her glass back and took a sip. Kathleen couldn't help but admire her long exquisite neck. An image of them naked in bed flashed through her mind, and she couldn't stop the burn of arousal that hit squarely in her groin. She should stop this, but she didn't want to.

"I need to be honest with you, Rebecca. I'm sort of in a relationship, but I find myself attracted to you."

"Define 'sort of in a relationship'."

"I have been with my partner for a number of years, but we were separated for eight months." Separated, although a true statement, wasn't exactly how she should define her partner of four years being abducted and held captive, raped, and tortured by a sadistic killer. Kathleen didn't really want to talk about Meredith's disappearance. She could only elude to their separation in vague terms. It didn't feel right. She hated lying, but she couldn't think of any other words to explain Meredith's absence from her life.

"We recently reunited, but things haven't been the same. She's different. I'm different. I think she knows, as much as I do, that our relationship is heading toward its end."

Rebecca reached out her hand and grasped Kathleen's. Her eyes practically smouldered in Kathleen's direction, which made Kathleen's pulse beat faster.

"We're just having fun, right? We don't need to swap life stories. Let's just enjoy the evening and see where it goes."

This was wrong, so very wrong, but Kathleen couldn't stop herself. She squeezed Rebecca's hand and took a gulp of her drink.

"I can do that."

The following morning, Kathleen put her key into Meredith's front door and walked in. Her gaze darted about the room, then settled on Meredith sitting on the couch. Kathleen shoved her hands into her pockets, knowing she looked rough and unkempt. She refused to meet Meredith's questioning gaze.

"Meredith, we need to talk," she said at length.

"Come into the lounge and sit down. Can I get you a drink?"

"No thank you, I'm fine." Kathleen walked fully into the room. She sat in the armchair, as far away from Meredith as she could get, and hesitantly looked at her partner. "I'm not sure how to tell you this, but you need to know what I have done."

Meredith didn't say anything. She crossed one leg over the other and folded her hands in her lap, apparently waiting for Kathleen to continue.

"I didn't go to London this weekend. I lied. I met a woman in a bar, and we slept together last night."

"Oh." Meredith blinked a few times, clearly in shock. "Tell me what's going on. Kath? I know you're struggling with everything that happened to me. Why didn't you talk to me?"

Meredith appeared calm in her questions and it threw Kathleen. How was she not up and yelling? "You've been through absolute hell, and I felt like a coward for not being able to help you. Just the thought of the things he did to you drives me crazy. I'm not emotionally equipped to deal with this, Meredith, and we are not the same people anymore. It's a callous thing to say, but you've changed, and I'm not the same person I was eight months ago either."

The quiet room made Kathleen squirm in her chair, looking everywhere but at the woman she was supposed to love.

"I know things have been a bit difficult for you," Meredith finally said. "But it hasn't exactly been a picnic for me either. I'm sorry that I didn't come home and just magically fall back into the person I was. You have to understand. The things I went through aren't something you just get over."

"Don't you think I know that? That's why I didn't say anything. I know you're facing a lot of demons. My feelings don't even compare to yours."

"So, you thought you would just go fuck someone else?"

"It wasn't like that, Meredith. I met her earlier in the week. We got along really well. It was nice to feel normal again, and not have to worry about kidnappers and rapists."

"Well, I'm glad you had a chance to escape for a while. I only wish I could afford myself the same luxury." Meredith rose from the sofa and headed toward the front door. "I can't believe, after all this time together, you could do this to me. Get out."

Kathleen stood and met her at the threshold. She wanted to reach out and touch her, offer her comfort, but she had no right, not now. She had thrown away everything for one night of passion with a stranger. "I'm sorry. I didn't mean for this to happen. I do love you, but maybe it's best if we just had a break for a while."

"I'm not sure I can forgive you for this. I need some time. I need to deal with Jaimeson West first," she said, referring to the man who had taken her against her will.

"I understand. Would it be okay if we keep in touch?"

"We'll see."

The slamming of the door made Kathleen jump. With her head hanging low, she made her way down the stairs and to her car. She sat for a full five minutes before driving away. She had screwed up, big time. There was no going back for them. Kathleen had hurt the one person who had loved her.

Self-loathing and a hard ball of guilt took up residence in her gut. She feared they would never leave her

CHAPTER ONE

August 2019

Kathleen stood in front of her full-length mirror, discouraged by what she saw. Her normally bright, shiny, blonde hair had lost its glory, looking flat and dull. Her once flawless skin was blotchy, with dark circles ringing her listless blue eyes. Endless nights of screwing strangers had replaced the restorative sleep she so needed and left her unable to focus properly at work. She had no one to blame but herself. Her betrayal of Meredith haunted her every waking moment, only fading when she was in the arms of a nameless woman. *That's what got me into this mess in the first place.* She shook her head. That wasn't completely true.

She had begun to distance herself the minute Meredith arrived home from the abduction that had nearly killed her.

Her mobile phone rang from its place on her night stand. "Hello?"

"Ms Scott, where are you?" David sounded harried.

"I'm at home. Why?" She ran her hand through matted hair, the after-effects of last night's alcohol making her fingers tremble.

"You're supposed to be in a meeting with the Mclean Group in ten minutes."

"That meeting isn't until the sixteenth." Kathleen blinked rapidly, trying to clear her foggy brain.

"That's today."

"What?" Her gaze darted around her bedroom, as if she expected to find herself in her office in London, not in her four-bedroom house on the outskirts of Bristol. "Oh shit. I'll have to do a conference call from my home office." Her thoughts raced as she tried to remember what the Mclean Group meeting was about.

Kathleen was a broker on the London Exchange and spent her time wooing clients to invest with the company that employed her. Mclean was a big fish in the corporate world. The manufacture of microprocessors gave them a lot of money to float on the market. If she didn't land this client, her job would be no more. Her boss had already given her a warning for tardiness, just one month ago, and he was looking for any excuse to fire her. Her job was all she had. She was damn good at it, well up until the last year. Her performance in the last twelve months was worse than when she'd started working for the company eight years ago.

Getting her mind back onto the problem at hand, she said, "Get them into the meeting room and set up the network link to my house. I'll need twenty minutes to get ready."

"Gerard isn't going to be happy about this, Kath," her assistant warned, as if she didn't already know.

"I know, but there isn't anything I can do about it now." A conference call was better than no meeting at all. She disconnected and threw her phone onto the unmade bed, where just two hours ago she'd been fucking some red head whose name she couldn't even begin to remember. *Did we even exchange names before I brought her back from the bar?*

There was no time to shower. She quickly scrubbed her face and applied some make-up. She tied her hair into a loose bun, hoping for the messy-on-purpose look and not the just-rolled-out-of-bed look, then slung on the cleanest trouser suit she could find from the washing hamper. *I thought today was Saturday already.* She'd planned on doing her laundry. Kathleen gave herself another beating over her recent life choices. An early morning meeting was the last thing she wanted to be doing.

She stubbed her toe as she ran into her office, cursing loudly, and switched on her computer. She connected to the office network and frantically pulled up the Mclean file. The clock in the corner of the monitor said she had seven minutes to scan the client's file. If she was lucky, she could bluff her way through the meeting.

†

Just after ten Monday morning, Kathleen stared out at the London's skyline from the window of her eleventh-floor office. She had yet to start any work. She could hear others rushing around and conversing with clients over the telephone and knew she should be doing the same. Instead, she sat with one leg crossed over the other, gently swivelling side to side in her chair. She hadn't even worn proper work attire. Her black jeans were just above casual and would be okay if she had no face to face meetings, but the baggy T-shirt shouldn't even be seen out of the home. Normally, she took great pride in her appearance. Her hair was always styled perfectly, and she would never be seen in anything but designer. Over the last twelve months, her worry about always looking put together had fled along with her drive and ambition. She just didn't see the point anymore. The world she'd so fiercely loved had become a sham. She hated her clients. She hated her boss. She hated sucking up to men in suits. More importantly, she hated herself. One mistake had smashed apart her world, and now the woman she loved was with someone else. *I wasn't there when she needed me the most.* Kathleen felt disgusted with herself.

A cough from the doorway caught her attention. She knew who it was before she even spun the chair around. "Good morning, Gerard." Her voice exposed her defeat. She had fucked up the meeting with the Mclean Group. She found she didn't actually care. She looked at her boss.

"Kathleen." His eyes were hard with disappointment. "I guess you know why I'm here."

She nodded.

He took a seat in the leather guest chair and loosened his tie, as if what he needed to say would be hard to get out with the noose tight around his thick neck. They stared at each other for a few moments, then Gerard's eyes softened.

"I don't really know what to say. When your partner was taken for eight months, you seemed to cope fine with work. In fact, you performed better than you ever had."

He was right. Those eight months were the most profitable in her career. Out-performing even the most senior staff had earned her a huge bonus. She had assumed Meredith was dead. What else could she do but work? No sense in wallowing, she had told herself. They had hardly ever seen each other anyway. Sure, they had keys to each other's houses and spent most weekends together, but they had both known it wouldn't have lasted. She did love Meredith, but she was never really *in love* with her. *I'm such an ass!*

"This last year, you have become worse. You're constantly late, rude to clients, and now you're not even dressed appropriately." He motioned to her T-shirt with a wave of his hand. "I can't allow what happened Friday to happen again, and I'm afraid it would." He took a deep breath. "I'm going to suspend you without pay, indefinitely, until you sort yourself out. I've arranged for David to work with Sandra and help transition your client list to her. I'm sorry, Kath, but you need to figure out what's going on in your head before I have to let you go permanently."

Well, there it was. She'd known it would come to this. If she was honest, she'd expected this months ago. She surmised her loyalty to the company had delayed the suspension. She stood from her chair, as did Gerard, and shook his hand over the desk. "I'm sorry, sir. I'll try not to take too long in figuring things out."

"Take as long as you need. You've earned this company a lot of money. I haven't forgotten that. Your job will be here when you get back." He nodded his head, then left.

Kathleen slumped back into her chair and faced the window again. *What the hell do I do now?* She couldn't muster any sadness over the suspension. Her heart hadn't been in work mode for a long time. It didn't matter they weren't going to pay her; she had made enough money over the last eight years to be comfortable for years to come. You didn't work that long in the stock market without learning a few things about investing your own money. No, she would be fine for cash, but what would she do to fill her time? *Soul search?* She laughed humourlessly. She wasn't even sure she had a soul anymore.

She gathered her things and headed to the parking garage under the office block. She would be back home by lunchtime, plenty of time to shower and change. She'd hit the town centre in the hopes of finding some company for the evening.

CHAPTER TWO

"Kathleen? Is that you?"

Kathleen dropped the pineapple back onto the pile in front of her, startled by Meredith's voice. She hadn't seen her for months and thought she never would again. They hadn't exactly left things on good terms. That was Kathleen's fault. Bracing herself, she turned around and stared. Meredith was as beautiful as ever. Her auburn hair shone, and the supermarket's overhead lights cast a bright glow around her head. The red and angry scar on her cheek was now barely visible. Life had come back to Meredith's eyes, and it made Kathleen want to cry. How could she have been so stupid to give her up?

"Mere. Hi." Kathleen felt chilled as Meredith's gaze roamed over her. *What must she be thinking?* Kathleen didn't have to wonder much longer.

"I don't want to be rude, but are you ill? You look terrible."

"Anyone ever tell you that you shouldn't say that to a woman?" Kathleen tried to laugh, but it came out as a sob. Before she knew what was happening, Meredith had gathered her in her arms, hugging her close. The familiar warmth of Meredith's embrace was intoxicating and made her cry all the more. "I'm so sorry, Meredith, about what I did and said."

"Hush. It's in the past." Meredith pulled back slightly, then wiped Kathleen's tears away with a brush of her thumb. "I have time if you want to talk."

Light reflected off a diamond ring on Meredith's finger. Kathleen grasped Meredith's hand and raised her eyebrows. "Steph?" Meredith nodded, smiling sadly. Stephanie Edwards had also been abducted, and that was when they had become friends. After the rescue, they'd kept in contact. Kathleen had hated Stephanie for a long time, blaming her for taking Meredith away from her, but she'd come to understand it was her fault alone. Kathleen had pushed Meredith away and into the arms of Stephanie, apparently allowing them to fall in love.

Meredith tugged Kathleen's hand, leading her to the exit. "There's a café around the corner. Let's go have a chat."

Kathleen saw no choice but to follow. Maybe it would be good to talk, to clear the air, perhaps then she would stop feeling so damn guilty all the time.

They entered Starbucks, and Meredith pushed her gently toward a table, then went to the counter to order. Kathleen sat down and watched Meredith scan the café, assessing everyone while she queued. Although it had been over a year since her rescue, she apparently still didn't like being out in public.

A few minutes later, Meredith returned with two mugs of steaming black coffee. "Thank you," Kathleen said.

"No problem." Meredith sat with her back to the wall, letting her keep an eye on her surroundings.

"I take it you don't like crowded places?"

Meredith raised her brows, eyes going wide. "How do you know that?"

"You keep looking around. Your gaze never stays on one thing for too long. You also face the room, so you can see what's going on."

"I'm doing a lot better than I was. I think I'll always be on the lookout for possible danger."

Kathleen took a sip of her drink to avoid commenting.

Meredith reached across the table and gently touched her arm. "What's going on, Kath? I've never seen you look so..."

"Unkempt?"

"I wouldn't say that." Meredith shook her head. "Lost sounds better."

Kathleen looked down at her tatty jumper and jogging bottoms. Meredith would never have seen her in public like this.

"It's not just your outfit," Meredith continued. "You look like you're sick. Tell me what's wrong."

Kathleen leaned back into her chair and folded her arms across her chest. How could she explain to Meredith that her life had fallen apart the day Meredith told her it was over for good and she loved Stephanie instead? Every day since,

Kathleen had tortured herself with guilt. It wasn't just the one-night stand. She hadn't been able to see Meredith's scars without feeling sick. She had failed to support her partner and had made her feel ashamed of what that guy had done to her. None of it was Meredith's fault. She didn't deserve to feel ugly or tainted. She deserved to be loved and cared for. *I hope she has that now, with Stephanie.*

She glanced up from the tabletop into Meredith's encouraging eyes. It was time to face the truth, to be honest, to apologise. She took a deep breath. "Meredith, I need to apologise for my behaviour after you came home—"

"It's okay."

"No, it's not. I should have been there for you, but I let my own selfish needs get in the way. I just couldn't cope with what happened." She lifted her hand to forestall Meredith's reply. "I felt loss and helplessness. I was horrified by what he'd done. But none of that should have mattered, because it was nothing compared to how you must have been feeling. I've felt guilty ever since then."

"This has been getting at you for the last year, hasn't it?"

"Yeah." She closed her eyes and shook her head. "I don't know what's wrong with me." As she opened them again, a tear ran down her cheek. "I've been suspended from work."

"What?"

"I haven't been doing my job properly. Messing up client meetings, missing deadlines. I spend most of my days staring into space, hating myself for what I did to you." She leaned forward, bracing her arms along the edge of the table. "What can I do to make it up to you? How can I make this better?" Meredith entwined their fingers, her warmth penetrating Kathleen's cold heart.

"You need to listen to me and listen good. You need to let it go. We both knew we were heading for a break-up anyway. The kidnapping just got in the way of that. You said some pretty nasty things to me, true, but I don't hold it against you. I forgave you, Kath, long ago. You need to do the same."

"I can't." More tears fell, but she didn't care that people were staring at them.

"You need to." Meredith stared at her for a few moments, a frown marring her features. "This is about more than the kidnapping and the aftermath, isn't it?"

How does she know that? Kathleen nodded. "I hate who I was, who I've become. I was so cold and superficial with you, with everyone. I don't want to be like that, but I'm afraid that's all I will ever be."

"The fact that you're here crying and questioning your past behaviour tells me you can change if you want to. But only you can do that. Stop thinking about who you were and concentrate on who you *can* be. I didn't love you because you were cold and superficial. You're a good person, you need to believe that."

Kathleen nodded again, although she didn't believe Meredith's words. She wasn't a good person, she only cared about herself. But she would try; she would find a way to change who she was, because she didn't want to end up alone.

She felt Meredith's ring touch her skin where their fingers were still linked together. A modicum of peace stole through her heart, knowing Meredith had found someone to make her happy. Kathleen looked up into her eyes. "You and Steph, she's good to you?"

A huge smile lit up Meredith's face. "She's amazing. We're getting married in three months."

Kathleen felt her lips stretch into a smile, even while jealousy slashed through her chest. Meredith was right. They had known they were heading for a break-up, but that didn't stop the what ifs from floating around Kathleen's head. "I'm happy for you, for you both."

"Thank you." Meredith looked away for a few seconds before she asked, "Maybe you could come?"

"To the wedding?"

She nodded. "Yeah."

That was quite possibly the worst idea on planet earth. Not only was Kathleen an emotional wreck at the moment but attending the wedding of her ex sounded awful. She highly doubted Stephanie would want her there. Every time they'd met, Stephanie looked like she wanted to kill her. *No way will I attend their wedding.* "We'll see," she said.

"Okay. I need to get going. I'm on the same number, if you ever want to talk."

"Thank you, but I think we both know that won't happen." Kathleen was mortified as it was that Meredith had seen her cry. One good thing had come out of this chance meeting; she had her forgiveness. She didn't know how much she had needed it until it was given.

They stood to leave, and Meredith leaned in and hugged her tightly. "I mean it, Kath. Just pick up the phone if you need to."

"Thank you," she whispered.

CHAPTER THREE

Bethany Jones strode across the main floor of Women with Hope Community Centre, or WHCC, at half past four, on her way to the small conference room at the back of the building. She had a meeting with the board of trustees, and she didn't want to be late. Her gaze quickly scanned the common room as she passed, glancing at the few women who were still milling about. WHCC opened its doors five years ago, and since then, the popularity of the place had grown and grown. The centre catered to all women, from all walks of life. Women who came here were in abusive relationships, on low incomes, or came just for a place to meet new people. Beth had been there since the beginning. She began as a support worker, then eventually earned a management role and was on call for women in crisis. Beth took her turn wearing many hats. She organised fundraising events, processed new arrivals, and helped the women get to their appointments. She even helped out with housekeeping. She loved her job and believed she would have found her way into working in the care community even without Darren's impact. She had a passion for helping people, and her own experience made it easier to recognise and understand other women in crisis.

The centre was only open nine to five, but an upstairs room was available twenty-four hours a day for women who needed somewhere to stay in an emergency. It wasn't a homeless shelter by any means, but an interim space offering a night or two of safety when women had nowhere else to go.

Beth nodded to the women as she passed through the door, which led to the kitchen and conference room. She rapped on the door once before entering. Four women sat behind the long table, paperwork in front of them. They all greeted Beth as she sat down. The unannounced meeting had caught Beth off guard. The board usually held monthly meetings with the three managers to make sure things were running smoothly and discuss any plans they had for upcoming events and the like. Their urgent request to meet with Beth had set her heart racing. She had racked her brain trying to figure out if she had done something wrong. There was nothing she could think of to warrant this meeting. She straightened her spine and wiped her sweaty palms on her thighs under the table.

"Ms. Jones, thank you for meeting with us," Director Margot Jeffords said. "You needn't look so worried. You're not in any trouble."

Beth blew out a quick breath, her anxiety lessening slightly.

"A few things came to light, during the annual audit, that gave us cause for concern."

WHCC was a charity that was run mainly on donations from businesses and subsidies from the city council. That's why they had the trustees, whose job was to make sure nothing nefarious was going on and who were all impartial to the running of the place. In essence, they were the gatekeepers but weren't allowed access themselves.

Margot continued. "As of twelve o'clock this afternoon, we have had to suspended Julie and Sarah." She sighed. "The auditor found some discrepancies in the accounts that need further investigation. It appears that funds have been misappropriated. So far, it looks like Julie and Sarah were behind it."

"What?" Beth couldn't quite get her head around this. Julie was the financial officer, and Sarah was the general manager of the whole place. They all worked closely together every day. Surely, she would have noticed if they had been stealing funds. "I hope you don't think—" Margot cut her off with a wave of her hand.

"We don't think you have any involvement. Your record is impeccable. We have spoken to other staff and learned that Julia and Sarah often stayed behind after hours. They are also close friends outside of work. Of course, that alone doesn't prove anything, but for reasons I can't get into, we know it comes down to them and not you."

Beth was pleased they didn't suspect her. *I couldn't stand to lose my job here. This place is my lifeline.*

"We also know you don't have access to any of the accounts or passwords." Margot smiled at her. "Your job is safe." She glanced down into the file in front of her. "Okay, to the matter at hand. As of tomorrow, we need you to add Sarah's duties to your own."

"Of course." It would mean more work for Beth, but she could handle it. She would call in extra volunteers to help cover the kitchen and the cleaning, and also more help with the fundraising. The rest she could do. Chloe was thirteen now, old enough to stay at home on her own if Beth had to work late. Chloe was used to Beth being called out in the middle of the night anyway, so it really wouldn't impact their life all that much.

"We obviously can't work with only one manager. We need to find a financial officer to cover Julie's role. We've put in a request for an interim until we can find a permanent replacement. Until we find someone, Diane will be overseeing things." Margot nodded across the table to the retired judge, who was in her sixties. "At some point, an investigator will need to talk to you about the goings-on, but you don't need to be worried. We trust you to take care of things until we get everything sorted.

"No problem. Thank you for your faith in me." Beth rose when Margot stood and reached across the table to shake her hand. "I'm really sorry about all this. I wish I had known."

"None of us did. I'm just pleased we insist on the annual audit. Otherwise, they could have gotten away with it for years."

Beth said her good nights and gathered her things. She headed out of the building, grateful that she wasn't on the night rotation. She had a lot to think over, planning out how she would effectively merge two jobs into one.

The car rolled to a stop in its usual spot around the back of the two-bedroom bungalow she lived in with Chloe. Home was a full thirty minutes from WHCC in the heart of Bristol, without any traffic delays. The sun had already begun its descent and cast a gloomy light around her.

As she locked the car and made her way around to the front of the building, an eerie feeling crept up her neck. She rubbed the spot where the hairs had risen and glanced around. There was no one in sight. She hastened her step. With another quick look over her shoulder, she unlocked the front door and stepped inside as fast as she could.

Beth leaned back against the door, her hand unconsciously going to the left side of her chest and shielding a three-inch scar. She hadn't thought about Darren for years, not seriously. Like an annoying itch you couldn't get rid of, he was always in her mind. She knew he would still be in prison, but the lingering feeling of being watched lingered.

"Hey, Mum."

Beth jumped.

Chloe was another reason Beth couldn't quite get Darren out of her head. Beth was five foot five, with mousy brown hair and brown eyes. She was slightly on the "puffy" side of average. Chloe looked like her father. The blue-eyed blonde was tall for a thirteen-year-old and lean. The only traces of Beth in Chloe were the full lips that always smiled beneath her straight, thin nose. Some days, Beth struggled to see any of herself in her daughter. It wasn't Chloe's fault her father turned out to be a monster. Beth would never make Chloe feel bad for the way she looked. Chloe was beautiful in her own right. Beth loved her, even if she saw Darren in her eyes.

"Hey, honey." She shed her coat and hung it up in the closet next to the door. "How was school?" Chloe flopped down on the sofa and began scrolling through her phone.

"It was all right."

Beth waited for more, but Chloe just continued to scroll. Beth sighed and walked through to the kitchen to start dinner. There was a time when she and Chloe would spend hours talking or watching TV together. Now, all Chloe wanted to do was chat with her friends and go on social media. *She is a teenager after all. At least she came out of her room to say hello, instead of shutting herself away in there like she does most of the time.*

CHAPTER FOUR

The Wednesday night group session would start at six o'clock. Beth entered a side room at WHCC, not as a staff member but as a client. The weekly meeting for survivors of domestic abuse had given her the support she needed to overcome the trauma. Thinking of the night Darren put her in the hospital always brought out a cold sweat. This night was no different. She was just glad Chloe hadn't been there that night. She had no doubt Darren would have hurt her too.

She walked over to the table that held the coffee urn and an assortment of cakes and biscuits. Beth dipped the tea bag in a mug of boiling water and glanced around the room. Seven or eight women had already claimed seats in the ring of chairs. She absently swirled a spoon through the splash of milk, as a familiar figure cut across her field of vision.

"Hey, Meredith."

"Hi." Meredith held a cup beneath the coffee urn and pressed the spigot handle.

Beth hadn't known Meredith long, just a few months, but they had become somewhat friendly. She didn't know a lot about Meredith's personal life but did know Meredith had been kidnapped and tortured. To Beth's mind, Meredith looked remarkably well, considering the hell she'd been through. *I would not have fared so well in that situation.*

"How has work been going?" Beth asked.

"It's a little slow, at the moment. The lead up to summer was good, but the darker evenings are closing in. We're finding clients are less likely to go property hunting."

Meredith was a high-end estate agent and did work all around the country. She had even found WHCC a new location for a branch they wanted to open in Weston-super-Mare. Beth idly wondered if the missing company funds would postpone the opening. She hoped not. It would be a shame to not have another branch available for women in crisis.

"That sucks."

"Yeah, but I have some ideas to help pick up business that will hopefully work out." The fine lines surrounding Meredith's eyes crinkled as she squinted slightly at Beth. "You look a little harried. Everything okay?"

No would be the short answer. The last two days had been hectic. Beth hadn't realised how much work went into being the general manager of the centre. She was always caught up in her own work hadn't given much thought to Sarah's responsibilities. *How did they even have time to steal from the company?* Beth barely had time to stop and breathe. It wasn't just the day-to-day running of the place she had to contend with. There were tons of paperwork, emails, appointments to see to, as well as coordinating groups and fundraising events. It had only been two days, and Beth was already behind. They needed to get some help, and fast. What made things harder was trying to get the funds released for anything like the weekly shopping or depositing a donation cheque. Without Sarah there to handle the money, Beth had to call Diane in from home to help her. Diane was only supposed to oversee things, but Beth couldn't do it all.

She glanced up and thought of blowing off Meredith's concern, but she wanted to talk to someone. Meredith was a friend, or at least becoming one. "Did you hear about Julie and Sarah?"

"Yeah, Francine is telling anyone who'll listen." Francine was the cook. She was in her early seventies and had volunteered at the shelter since her husband passed away. She was a lovely woman but the biggest gossip. Beth shook her head.

"Well, things have been crazy busy since Monday. The trustees put me in charge of running everything, but I don't think I can keep up. I was busy enough doing my own work, but now I find myself trying to take on all three jobs."

Meredith reached out and squeezed her forearm in sympathy. "What are they doing about finding replacements?"

"Margot's put the feelers out for a financial officer. Diane is covering for now, but she can't be here full time. We've got adverts out for more volunteers to help with the load but so far haven't had any interest."

Meredith looked away for a second, her forehead creasing. "I know someone who might be able to help you."

"Really? Who?" Beth raised her brows, hoping this was good news.

"Her name is Kathleen. She usually works on the stock exchange, but she's currently taking a sabbatical." Meredith had stumbled over the last word. If Beth didn't have such a good read on people, she may have missed it. There was something about the look in Meredith's face that had Beth questioning whether this would be a good idea.

"Sabbatical?" she questioned. Beth knew, without doubt, this wasn't just a case of time off work. There was something else going on. *Is it my place to judge?*

Meredith touched her arm again. "I swear, she's trustworthy. She's just spent a long time working with no real time off. She needed a break, but she isn't the type to just sit around and do nothing for months. I think she'd be perfect, while the trustees search for a more permanent replacement for Julie."

Beth thought for a moment. It would be a great help if this Kathleen stepped in for a while. If there was anything bad in her history, it would come up when they ran her background check. Margot wouldn't let anyone work at WHCC without checking them fully. Beth also knew Meredith wouldn't have suggested Kathleen if there was something amiss with her.

"Give me her details, and I'll talk to Margot in the morning."

Meredith nodded and smiled. "Okay. It looks like we're ready to start." She indicated June, the woman who would be moderating the group. They found their seats, and Beth tried to listen to the women talk, but she found herself wondering if she had just made a mistake. Meredith didn't seem entirely sure about suggesting Kathleen. Beth's mind whirled at what might have caused the hesitation in her recommendation and why Kathleen was no longer at work.

†

Kathleen swallowed the last of her merlot, then slid the empty glass onto the oak coffee table in front of her. She leaned back into the sofa, crossing her arms over her belly and staring at the ceiling. She had been off work for three weeks, and she had accomplished nothing. The furthest she went from home was to the shops to buy wine and takeout. She hadn't even mustered the energy to go on the prowl for some nameless woman who wouldn't mind hooking up. Her passion for anything had vanished. She didn't know how she was supposed to get her head on straight when all she did was sleep, drink, and stare into space. She had thought about trying to go back to work, but she knew Gerard wouldn't allow it. He would see she hadn't changed in the last three weeks and refuse her.

She stood and padded into the kitchen, her feet chilling as they touched the slate floor. She opened the fridge, but nothing took her fancy. She slammed the door, then eyed the wine rack. The three bottles taunted her where she stood. She needed to be careful. She was on the verge of having a problem. If she started down that route, then she would have no hope of finding her way back to who she was.

Kathleen turned her back on the wine and the kitchen, deciding a soak in the bath would probably be a better option. As she passed through the living room, her landline rang from the end table. *Odd. No one calls that number anymore.* She wasn't even sure why she still had it plugged in. She picked up the receiver.

"Hello?"

"Kath, is that you?"

Kathleen blinked a few times, her hand tightening around the phone. She hadn't expected to hear from Meredith again. "Mere? Why are you calling? Wait, that sounded rude. I'm just surprised." She leaned back on to the arm of the sofa, the sound of Meredith's voice making her heart trip. One thing Meredith could always do was turn her on with the sound of her voice. Kathleen closed her eyes and tried to dispel the flood of memories. Meredith wasn't hers anymore, and Kathleen had no right to think of her in that way.

"I'm sorry, it's late. I hope you don't mind me calling."

"No, it's fine. What can I help you with?"

"Um, are you still on leave from work?"

Kathleen frowned, wondering why she wanted to know that. "Yes. I'm not sure when, or if, I'll be back." She hated saying those words out loud, admitting her failure, but maybe that was the best way to start getting back on track. "Why?"

"I kinda gave someone your number. They should be calling you in regard to a job."

"Wait, what? Mere, I'm supposed to be taking time to 'find' myself, not working another job."

"I know, but I also know you have a hard time sitting still. The women's centre I go to needs an interim financial officer, while they look for a permanent replacement. They had some funds go missing, and two of the staff are under investigation. They need help. I thought, while you're not working in London, you could help them out."

Kathleen said nothing as she processed what Meredith had said. For one, she had no idea Meredith was going to a women's centre. She realised it was none of her business. But two, why on earth would Meredith think Kathleen would want to work for a women's centre? She hadn't been able to help Meredith when she'd needed her. Why, how, would she be able to face God knows who suffering from God knows what.

"I know what you're thinking, but it isn't that kind of centre. Yes, they do have abused women there, but it's mainly a place where women can go to hang out, make friends, do activities, and receive help and information. It's a charity. Beth, the woman who is running it now, needs help. Please, Kath, just give it a go."

"Why are you so desperate to get me to help? I'm useless at that sort of thing, as well you know." She didn't want to make that remark, but she needed to remind Meredith she was talking to a cold-hearted bitch who didn't care about anyone, let alone a bunch of strangers with family problems and the like. She heard Meredith sigh down the line.

"Look, Kath, I know you're in a bad place right now. Maybe helping those less fortunate than you might do you some good."

So, in other words, stop being a selfish cow and think about others for a change. Wasn't that what Kathleen wanted to do? Wasn't that why she felt so guilty over hurting Meredith, because she hadn't helped her as she should have? Kathleen ran her fingers along the edge of the table. Perhaps, if she hadn't had a bottle of wine, she might have been able to resist.

"Okay… If they call and want to set up an appointment, I promise I'll go."

"That's great," Meredith enthused. "I really do think you'll get something out of this, Kath, you'll see."

"Yeah, right."

Kathleen put the receiver down and went back into the kitchen. The hot bath now forgotten, she pulled out another merlot. *What have I just gotten myself into?*

CHAPTER FIVE

The following Monday morning, Kathleen found herself sitting in a small office on the first floor of Women with Hope Community Centre, dressed in her best skirt suit, hair pinned up and make-up applied. She still didn't know what she had been thinking, telling Meredith she would interview for the job. Getting dressed that morning had felt strange and uncomfortable. It had been so long since she'd dressed with any sense of pride, that putting on the clothes and make-up made her feel like an imposter. *I'm here now. Let's see what happens.*

Director Margot Jeffords looked to be in her mid-fifties with a formidable presence. Her greying hair was cut stylishly around her oval face. Her brown eyes were dark and focused. *Whatever Margot's profession, she must be a very powerful figure.* Kathleen knew that she also possessed that same air of confidence. Well, she had, before everything turned to shit.

"So, Ms Bowden-Scott, from what I can see of your credentials, you appear to be a good fit for the charity."

"Thank you. And please, call me Kath."

Margot smiled. "Okay, Kath. We will obviously need to get a criminal records check done and speak to your last employer, just to make sure everything is on the up and up."

This was the one thing Kathleen had been dreading. She would have to explain why she was no longer working for Gerard. She glanced away for a moment. Honesty was probably the best option. Margot would find out from Gerard anyway. Kathleen cleared her throat.

"I do need to clarify why I'm currently taking a break from working for Gerard's firm."

Margot raised her eyebrows and folded her hands together on the desk. She leaned forward ever so slightly. Kathleen's heart raced, and she mustered all her energy toward not letting her anxiety show.

"About two years ago my partner was abducted for eight months." She refrained from saying Meredith's name, not wanting to discuss her business with a woman who was essentially a stranger. There was a good chance Margot already knew Meredith, as she came to the centre. Still, it wasn't Kathleen's place to say. "I didn't handle her homecoming particularly well, and we broke up. Over the last year, things came to a head. I found I was losing concentration at work. Gerard thought it best I take a break and return when I'm feeling better." She leaned back in her chair and waited for Margot to dismiss her, because she would. Kathleen was a walking liability.

Margot studied her face for a long moment. "I can't imagine any of what you went through was easy. I can understand you needing to take time to heal."

Heal? What on earth was she talking about? Meredith was the one who needed to heal, not Kathleen. She hadn't been through anything, apart from half the lesbians in Bristol. She refrained from commenting.

"WHCC is under a lot of strain right now. Unfortunately, we can't continue to run on the staff we have. If you can promise me that you will come to me if you begin to struggle, I don't see a problem with you helping us out until we can find a permanent solution."

Kathleen was dumbfounded. She hadn't expected compassion or even simple acceptance. She cleared her throat, pleased when her voice came out normal. "I appreciate that. I swear, the minute I feel I'm letting the charity down, I'll let you know."

"Great." Margot closed the folder she had been leafing through and relaxed her posture, taking on a more friendly demeanour. "Let me tell you a little about the place. The building is two thousand square feet over two levels. The ground floor houses our conference room, main hall, kitchen, and two smaller rooms for groups or gatherings. The first floor is set up with the cots we use for emergency housing or crisis." Margot gestured with open palms. "This is the trustee's office. Your office, the day manager's and the events managers are also here on the ground floor. We open the doors, officially, nine to five, but we are staffed twenty-four-seven if someone needs a bed for the night. The staff and volunteers rotate the night shifts through the week. We wouldn't expect you to do that though, not being trained for crisis.

"Your duties will be handling the accounts and funds. If anything needs paying for, that will be your department. You'll also be in charge of allocating monies and funds for events and the like. We usually do three big fundraising events per year, and we have one coming up in three months. As you're aware, we have had some funds go missing. So, this event won't be as big as we would like. I'll need you to work with Beth to scrape up as much money as you can to put on the event."

"That all sounds fine." Kathleen was used to working with hundreds of thousands of pounds. Running one small charity wouldn't be a problem; she could do it in her sleep.

"As for your salary–"

"I don't need one"

"Excuse me?"

"You don't need to pay me. I'm financially stable. I'd rather you used the money for the charity."

Shock clearly showed in Margot's features and wide eyes. "Are you sure?"

"Yes." She nodded. "I wasn't planning on working for a while anyway. I'm glad to help you out as much as I can."

"Well, that's certainly generous. I should really argue with you about that, but I'd be a fool to turn your offer down. Thank you."

"No problem."

"I think that covers everything then. I'll give you a quick tour of the place, then show you to your new office. Diane will be in later to take you through everything. You can spend some time getting to know the systems before starting tomorrow."

"Perfect."

They both stood, and Kathleen followed Margot around as she showed her the centre, introducing her to the other staff members and a few clients as they went. They stood by the kitchen, discussing the bulletin board, when they were interrupted by a loud crash. The expletive from behind the double doors would have made a sailor blush.

"Bloody hell, Fran, it's gone everywhere."

"Sorry, boss."

"Excuse me." Margot blushed at the exchange of words, obviously not pleased bad language had been used in front of a new employee.

Kathleen couldn't help but follow Margot through the doors to see what had happened. She stepped through and had to bite her lip at the scene in front of her. A medium-height woman with light brown, wavy hair held a sodden T-shirt away from her body. What looked like tomato soup dripped steadily onto the floor. An older lady was trying to wipe it off the poor woman.

"I'm sorry, Beth." The older woman looked like she would cry any minute.

"It's fine."

Margot stepped over the puddle of soup to Beth's side and grasped the hem of her shirt. "You need to take that off before it burns your skin." For a moment, Beth looked truly mortified that Margot was about to strip her. She quickly schooled her features.

"I'll go to the toilets and clean myself off." She sidestepped Margot.

In her haste, she stepped on the soup and slipped. Her arms flailed, and she pitched forward. Kathleen didn't have time to think. She reached her arms out and caught the woman before she fell face first onto the tiled floor. Kathleen held her firm against her body, and her only thought was that she had ruined her best suit. The woman, Beth, looked up. Her cheeks were tinged with red, and Kathleen felt she had just been kicked in the gut. Beth was beautiful, even with soup dripping from the ends of her hair. Her brown eyes glistened, and Kathleen noticed a tiny fleck in one of her irises. Rounded cheeks swooped down to a pointed chin, her lips full and rose coloured. One small dimple stood out in her right cheek, and she looked absolutely adorable. Kathleen's hands unconsciously tightened on the woman's biceps. She couldn't help but hold on longer, even when she knew Beth had righted herself and was standing on her own.

"Excuse me," Beth muttered as she looked away.

Kathleen dropped her hands. Beth scurried around her and out the door. If that was who she would be working with, she would have a hard time concentrating. *Maybe working here wouldn't be so bad after all.*

"Fran, get a mop," Margot requested.

"I'll do it," Kathleen heard herself say.

"No, it's okay, I don't need help cleaning up my mess."

Kathleen thought that was rather abrupt but stopped herself from insisting. Francine obviously didn't want her help, and she wouldn't push. It was then she noticed her blouse was sticking to her skin and remembered the soup Beth had transferred onto Kathleen's outfit. She pursed her lips in a frown at the mess of her Gucci suit. "I need to go home and change."

"Nonsense," Margot replied. "We have plenty of stuff you can change into. You don't need to be driving around looking like that. Follow me. I'll get you something."

Kathleen didn't really have a choice, as Margot stepped back over the soup and through the door.

37

†

Beth held her wet T-shirt under the hand dryer, her body still registering a thrum of anxiety at the thought of Margot reaching for her shirt. It was no secret that Darren had attacked and stabbed her, but no one had seen the scars. She wasn't ashamed of them, however, that didn't mean she wanted to be a sideshow in her place of work.

The toilet door opened, and Beth glanced over her shoulder. The woman she assumed to be Kathleen stood just inside. If it wasn't bad enough she had been covered head to toe in soup, she had then slipped into the arms of a stranger. And that was disquieting too. She hadn't had a relationship since Darren, and everyone knew to respect her personal space. She had no idea how she would feel when someone held her, but it certainly wasn't the rush of arousal that shot through her body as this stranger pulled her into her body. Beth chalked it up to the adrenalin of nearly face planting the floor, and not the blue eyes that sparkled with mischief, or the heady scent of her perfume.

"Uh, sorry," Kathleen said. "I didn't know anyone was in here."

"That's okay." Beth tried to cover herself with her T-shirt, but not before Kathleen's gaze slipped lower, onto her chest. Kathleen's eyes suddenly widened. Beth turned her back, forgetting the larger scar on her shoulder blade. She heard Kathleen's whispered "Jesus." Beth lowered her head. She hadn't wanted anyone to ever see her scars, and now a stranger had seen all of them. Her eyes teared and she frantically tried to find the bottom of her shirt so she could yank it on. Her humiliation, it seemed, could get worse.

"Here."

38

Beth looked back. Kathleen was holding open a T-shirt Margot must have given her to change into. She noticed that Kathleen didn't lower her gaze, giving her a modicum of privacy.

"Thank you." Beth raised her arms and allowed Kathleen to pull the shirt over her head.

"No problem." Kathleen stepped back, slipping her hands into the pockets of her jacket. "I'm Kathleen, by the way."

"I figured." She held out her hand, her fingers shaking. "Beth."

"Nice to meet you."

"I'm, ah, sorry about your suit." Beth's gaze roamed over the very expensive-looking skirt suit. She didn't know a lot about fashion, but even she could tell it wasn't cheap. And now it was sporting soup. "If you send me the cleaning bill, I'll take care of it."

Kathleen waved her hand in the air. "It's fine. It's just clothing."

Beth raised her eyebrows. She had no doubt the suit cost an entire week's wage.

A few beats of silence stretched between them, Beth could see the questions in Kathleen's eyes and wanted to be anywhere but in this restroom. She had no reason to hide. Everyone knew, and it wouldn't be long before Fran or another gossip told Kathleen anyway. At least this way Beth could control the flow of information. She pointed to her chest, indicating the scars beneath her shirt.

"My ex-husband didn't like my request for a divorce."

Kathleen didn't say anything. For a second, Beth thought she hadn't heard, but Kathleen's lips pursed. Her brows pinched, causing little wrinkles to deepen between them. She nodded slowly but still didn't answer. Beth's heart beat wildly in her chest, as she waited for Kathleen to say something, anything. Kathleen briefly closed her eyes, and when she opened them Beth swore she could see a hint of sympathy. It was gone in a flash.

"I need to find Margot," Kathleen said. "To find something else to wear. It was nice meeting you." She turned on her heel and strode away.

Beth fell back against the tiled wall, the cold penetrating her T-shirt. She felt bereft. She had never experienced the brutal rejection she had just felt from Kathleen's dismissal. She knew the scars were ugly, but she thought Kathleen would have at least acknowledged their existence. She didn't want, or need, sympathy from her, but to completely ignore Beth's admission, and the anguish she felt over saying the words tore through her. She should have just put the T-shirt on and excused herself, she didn't need to explain anything to Kathleen, a stranger.

Feeling like a complete idiot for opening herself up, she gathered her damp T-shirt and went to her office, ignoring anyone who greeted her. She needed time to slip her mask back in place before she had to face Kathleen again. The last thing she wanted was to appear weak in front of someone who seemed to have complete control over their life.

†

Kathleen said goodbye to Diane, then slouched back into her ergonomic office chair. She hadn't realised how much went into running a charity like this. Diane had gone through the computer and filing system, the bank accounts, and passwords. Kathleen was an intelligent woman, but even she had a hard time keeping up. She thought maybe her lack of concentration over the last year had something to do with it. She had no worries, though. She would look over it all again before she went home, first thing tomorrow, she'd start working on an action plan to sort everything out. Sarah had done a good job of messing up the accounts, and Kathleen now had to run the charity on a strict budget until the investigation could be sorted and the rest of their funds could be released. It wasn't good news for the centre, and Kathleen didn't think Beth would be happy with the news some services would need to be cut. She didn't relish that conversation.

Kathleen thought back to earlier that morning when she had walked into the restroom. Seeing Beth half-dressed had been a welcome surprise, until she'd caught sight of the large scar on her chest, just above her heart. For a moment, she thought Beth had had heart surgery or something. However, when Beth had turned her back the jagged, eight-inch scar across her shoulder blade told her something horrific had happened.

She hadn't been prepared when Beth's eyes teared and she casually relayed what her husband had done. How was Kathleen supposed to respond to that? She wanted to ask a myriad of questions, but her mouth wouldn't work. All she could do was stare stupidly until she made her legs work and ran out of there. She could still feel the anger bubbling inside her at the mere thought of anyone doing that to someone who seemed as sweet as Beth.

Kathleen knew, deep down, she was ill-equipped to deal with Beth's trauma. She hadn't been able to support her partner of four years after she went through something horrific. No way would she be able to offer anything to someone she'd just met. She probably owed Beth an apology for her abrupt departure, but how could she do that when she didn't know what to say? She needed to figure something out. and soon. No doubt, she would be seeing Beth again tomorrow.

CHAPTER SIX

The following morning, Kathleen looked up from the accounts she was working on when she heard a rap on her door. Beth stood in her open doorway, fidgeting from foot to foot.

"Morning," Kathleen said, trying to relax her face to appear friendly and open. She still didn't know how she was going to apologise for yesterday. Throughout the evening, while working on an action plan, her mind had constantly travelled back to Beth and the scars she had seen. She could only imagine the terror she must have felt when her husband had attacked her. The violence that someone could inflict on a loved one turned her stomach. It was the same with Meredith. Kathleen just couldn't process the trauma Meredith had experienced being abducted and tortured, so she ran. She wished she was better equipped to deal with this sort of thing. She had no business helping out at the centre, where most of the women were in crisis. *Well, I'm here now.* She was determined not to let them down.

"Good morning, Kathleen. Um, is now a good time to go over the budget for the fundraising event?"

Kathleen didn't like the look of shame on Beth's face, knowing she had put it there. She sighed, then stood. She came around the desk and stepped toward Beth. "Now is fine. Please, take a seat." Beth did as asked, and Kathleen closed the door. She sat back in her seat and took a breath. "Before we discuss the budget, I feel I need to apologise to you for yesterday."

"No, it's fine."

Kathleen didn't believe that for a second. Beth still hadn't looked her in the eye, and Kathleen could see fresh tears moistening her eyes. She blew out a breath. She stood again and knelt by Beth's chair, placing her hand on the arm to steady herself. She dipped her head and tried to catch Beth's eye, pleased when she did.

"It's not fine. I reacted poorly. You've obviously been through hell, and I made you feel bad about it. I'm sorry. It was just a shock. I'm not very good at dealing with this sort of thing, but I'm trying to get better."

Beth stared at her for a moment, then her lips stretched into a small smile. "It really is okay. I was a little upset, but we don't know each other. You don't owe me anything, especially sympathy, for things we can't change."

"Still, I'm sorry."

Beth's smile grew wider and she nodded. Kathleen was forgiven. She was pleased she had been able to defuse the situation with Beth before it got totally out of hand. Her knees cracked as stood and returned to her seat. She glanced at the accounts again and knew she would be upsetting Beth for the second time in two days.

"As you know, the accounts have been suspended, pending an investigation. We have been allowed a modicum of funds to keep the centre running. I've been looking over the services we run and seeing where we can save money, until such time the accounts are unfrozen." She looked up at Beth and steeled herself for the outburst that was about to come. "We need to do some major restructuring, starting with the evening groups and the night shelter."

"What?" Beth exploded.

"We just don't have the funds to pay two people to stay on at night in case someone wants to come in. From what I've seen, you've only had four overnight clients in the last three weeks. That's three weeks of wages lost."

"We might not have someone need us every night, but we still need to have that facility in case we do."

"I'm sorry, the money is just not there, not at the moment." Kathleen watched, as Beth tried to control her breathing. She was pissed. Her cheeks were flaming, and her nostrils flared repeatedly. Kathleen understood the need for the services they provided, but the money wasn't there to provide them. She couldn't help that. She was here to run the finances, and she would do it how she saw fit.

"What about the groups?" Beth asked through gritted teeth. Her anger was flowing off her in waves.

"Again, it comes down to costs. We have to pay for refreshments and utility bills for the extra opening times, as well as a staff member to stay late five nights a week. If you can fit them into our normal operating hours, then fine. Otherwise they need to be suspended."

"Do you have any idea about what we do here?" Beth stood from her chair then leaned forward onto the desk, forcing Kathleen to look up at her. "These women need this place. They can't pick and choose when their husband will attack them, or when they find themselves homeless. They need the groups to help them socialise, to find a place they can be safe and talk about things that hurt them. You can't come in here and just stop it all just to save a few quid."

Kathleen didn't look away from Beth's face, enthralled by her beauty when she was angry. That didn't stop her reply. "I can, and I will. The trustees have put me in charge of financing. I can't give you what we don't have."

"How can you be so cold?"

Now that stung, but wasn't it the truth? Kathleen didn't get this far in business playing nice and bending over at the first sign of trouble. She set her jaw. "Because I have to be."

They glared at each other for a long moment. Kathleen refused to look away first. Eventually, Beth sunk back in her chair with a shuddering breath.

"I'll run the groups," Beth said, "as a volunteer. That will save you some money. Take the utilities from my wages. I'm not giving them up."

Kathleen was impressed. Not many people would be willing to sacrifice their time and money to help others. It was clear Beth really cared about this place and the women in it.

"As for the night shifts, I'll put a business card by the door. If someone needs us, they can call me, and I'll come stay. Free of charge, of course." She smiled sweetly at Kathleen. "The women come first, always."

Kathleen nodded. She couldn't stop Beth doing what she wanted. Beth was now the centre manager. If she wanted to spend her time running around after everyone, that was her prerogative.

"Do you have any idea what fundraising event you'll be doing?"

"Not yet." Beth shook her head "The event planner is waiting to see what our budget is first. He knows we'll be short. This is usually our biggest event of the year, when we get the most donations. But if we can't have the funds to organise it, we won't get the turnout we need."

"How much do you usually spend?" Kathleen could hear the pleading in Beth's voice. She hated to anger her again, but she had no choice.

"Between three and four thousand, depending on the venue et cetera."

Kathleen looked at the account ledger. She had pencilled in five hundred pounds for the event, and that was stretching the funds thin. She glanced back up to Beth's brown eyes full of hope. Kathleen shook her head.

"The most I can give you is five hundred." She waited for the explosion, but it never came. Beth just lowered her head, shoulders slumped. "I really am sorry, Beth. If the investigation gets cleared up soon, then maybe we'll have the funds."

Beth looked up, unshed tears in her eyes. "We both know investigations like this take months. We need to start planning now and paying for things, otherwise the event won't happen. If we can't do the event, we won't get the donations we need to stay open. This event usually sets us up for a good six months' worth of running costs. If we can't do it, we'll have to close. There is only so much the council is willing to set aside for us."

Kathleen closed her eyes and sighed heavily. She couldn't take looking into Beth's wounded expression any longer. Five grand wasn't really that much money. Was it? Not when you could comfortably live off your investments for the rest of your life. She knew she didn't have a choice. She couldn't stand by, day after day, and let the place fall apart all the while she had six figures sitting in her bank.

"I'll pay for it," she said quietly, then opened her eyes.

"What?"

Kathleen sat straighter in her chair and cleared her throat. "I'll make a donation of five thousand pounds to be used exclusively for the fundraising event."

"Why would you do that?" Beth stared at her; eyes wide.

"I've made a pretty bad impression on you already. This might help you hate me less for everything else I have to take away." Kathleen shrugged. She couldn't very well tell her it was Beth's wounded eyes that broke her heart and made her want to comfort and help her.

"So, a bribe then, to stop me nagging you?"

Kathleen thought for a moment that Beth was serious but then saw the slight gleam in her eyes. She smiled back. "I think I'll need more than that to stop you nagging me."

Beth was about to reply when her mobile beeped. "Sorry." She pulled the phone from her pocket and read the text. Kathleen noticed the colour drain from Beth's face and her trembling hands. She quickly stood from the desk and rushed to Beth's side, instinctively knowing something bad had happened.

"What's the matter?" She crouched and touched Beth's shoulder. Beth passed the phone to her and Kathleen read the email. She lifted her gaze back to Beth, not sure what she had just read.

"My ex. He's been let out of prison early for good behaviour." The words came out forced, devoid of emotion.

It wasn't hard to miss the terror in Beth's eyes. Kathleen didn't know what to do. "Does he know where you are?"

Beth shook her head. "I don't think so. We moved from Yorkshire as soon as I got out of the hospital. I need to get a restraining order. And I need to tell Chloe." At Kathleen's raised eyebrows, she clarified, "My daughter."

Kathleen nodded. "If you need to leave, I'm sure the guys can handle everything until you get back."

"Are you sure?"

"Of course. Go."

"Thank you."

They stood and Kathleen walked her to the door. "Um, let me know if there is anything I can do." The words came out strange, even to Kathleen's ears. She wasn't kidding when she said she sucked at these kinds of things. She knew business and numbers. Everything else was foreign to her, but she didn't like the idea of Beth dealing with this on her own. Then again, Beth never said she was on her own. For all Kathleen knew, Beth had another husband and was happily married. Her gaze involuntarily went to Beth's hand. No ring. Didn't mean she wasn't involved with someone. *Why am I even thinking about this now? Beth is in the middle of a crisis. I really am a jerk.*

"I'll be back as soon as I can."

"Take your time. We'll be fine." Kathleen hoped that was true. With Beth gone, she was the next in command.

†

Beth paced anxiously in the outer room of Benson and Conner, waiting to see her solicitor. She didn't have an appointment, but she couldn't wait for one to be made available. She needed to see him now. Why was Darren released early and why hadn't she been warned? She needed to find out how to make a restraining order. She didn't want Darren coming anywhere near her. Her heart rate hadn't settled since the moment she received the email an hour ago. She couldn't believe he was out, free to finish her off, if he so pleased.

Before she had a chance to work herself up more than she already was, the door to Graham Willis's office opened and he stepped out, an apologetic smile stretching his thin lips.

"Ms Jones, sorry to keep you. Come on in." Beth followed behind and settled in his guest chair. Graham took his seat and folded his hands together on top of his mahogany desk. "What can I do for you?"

"I want to know why Darren has been let out of prison already." She had to concentrate on keeping her voice steady. Her fear of Darren nearly made her throat close over.

Graham turned slightly in his chair and typed into his keyboard. After a moment of looking at his monitor, he took a breath. "From what I can gather from the court records, he was released because of good behaviour. Since he was put away, he has been a model prisoner. He maintained a job in the kitchen and hasn't gotten into any trouble. The parole board feels he has been rehabilitated."

"He got ten years minimum. How can they let him out after five?"

Graham shrugged. "Prisons are overcrowded. If he proved he was sorry for his crime and doesn't seem to be a threat anymore, they feel he's okay to go back into society."

"That's crazy," she exclaimed. "He put me in the hospital for a month. I'm lucky I'm alive." This all felt like a nightmare. She had only just begun to get her life back, finally feeling safe in her environment. She didn't want to spend the rest of her life looking over her shoulder. "What about Chloe?"

Graham's brows furrowed, his lips turning down slightly in the corners. "From a legal standpoint, he has every right to see her. He didn't harm her in any way, so he could argue his parental rights should still be in force."

"No way is he getting near her."

"He's been released on probation and a restraining order is already in place. He's not allowed near you. Any visits with your daughter would be supervised."

"We have to do something to stop him. I can't let him see her." Beth jumped up from the chair.

"Ms Jones, I'm sorry, but if he wants to see her, we can't stop him."

Beth leaned over the desk, making direct eye contact with him. "Find a way. I'll go into hiding before I let that monster anywhere near me and my family."

Graham stared back at her for a moment, then shook his head imperceptibly. "I'll see if there is anything I can do, but I can't make any promises."

She nodded her thanks, but his attempt to placate her didn't do anything to settle her anxiety. No legal action could stop Darren if he wanted to hurt her. She didn't think spending five years in prison would be enough to assuage his anger at her wanting to leave him. If anything, it probably made him worse. She had lived with him long enough to know how resentful he could be.

51

"Do you know where he is?" Beth settled back into her chair. If he was living anywhere near Bristol, she would need to make plans to leave. Just being in the same country was enough to turn her stomach. She may have changed her name, but you could find out anything if you had the right amount of money. She wouldn't wait around to be found.

Graham looked at his monitor again. "The parole board has him living back in Yorkshire. He won't be allowed to leave the county, and he's on electronic tagging for six months. You're perfectly safe."

He smiled reassuringly at Beth, but it didn't help. Darren was an attempted murderer. One ankle bracelet wouldn't stop him if he wanted to get to her. She said her goodbyes and headed for her car. She would need to collect Chloe early from school and explain her dad was out...and probably looking for them.

†

"I don't get what's going on, Mum." Chloe stormed through the front door into the lounge and threw her school bag onto the couch. She spun on her heel and glared at Beth. "I was in the middle of a test."

Beth closed the front door and went to Chloe, taking her hands in her own. She had left Graham's office and went straight to Chloe's high school. She told the headteacher she needed to pull Chloe from her lesson due to a family emergency. She didn't elaborate, and the head wasn't pleased about allowing his student to miss the exam she was taking. Beth didn't care. If Chloe had been sitting her final exams, she might have been more hesitant about dragging her out of school. The practice test wasn't important to Chloe's future.

Besides, if Darren was heading in their direction, Chloe wouldn't be staying at the school anyway.

"I'm sorry, honey, but I needed to talk to you about something really important. I couldn't do that at school."

Beth moved Chloe's bag onto the floor. She settled on the sofa, pulling Chloe with her. She kept hold of Chloe's hand, wanting the connection to her. Chloe had only been eight years old when Darren attacked Beth. She had been staying at a friend's house, and Beth thought that was the perfect opportunity to tell Darren she was leaving him. She knew he wouldn't be happy about it. He was always trying to control her, but she never expected him to try and kill her. After the attack, he did a runner.

When the friend's mum dropped Chloe off the next morning, they found Beth lying in her own blood, unconscious and very near death. Beth hated that Cloe had been the one to find her.

Chloe hadn't spoken much about the attack over the years. Beth wondered what seeing her like that would cost Chloe, growing up. So far, Chloe was a normal sullen teenager. Beth had hoped it would stay that way, but news of Darren's release made that a false hope.

"You're making me worried, Mum. What's happened?"

Beth took a deep breath, trying to steady her racing heart. "Honey, I received an email from my solicitor this morning. Your father has been released from prison." Beth waited for the litany of questions, but they never came. Chloe sat ramrod straight, staring at her. "Honey, did you hear what I said?"

Chloe nodded slowly. "Yeah."

"How do you feel about that?"

Chloe shrugged. She looked away for a moment then back at Beth. "Can I go to my room? I've got homework to do."

Beth sighed and nodded. "Of course." She didn't know what she'd expected. Chloe's lack of any emotion worried her. If Chloe was anything like Beth, she probably needed time to process everything. They would need to talk properly about this at some point. Soon. Beth would need Chloe to understand there was a good chance they would be moving. She would no longer be allowed to stay away a night at friends' houses. Chloe's social life was about to take a nosedive.

That wasn't Beth's only problem. She had the centre to think of. She had just agreed to be the sole night shift worker and run the evening groups. There was no way she could leave Chloe at home while she was at work. Chloe wouldn't be happy, but she would have to accompany Beth to the centre, when she wasn't at school. Beth didn't like the thought of having to wake Chloe up during the night. She knew it would disrupt her schooling, but she didn't have a choice. Until she knew they were safe from Darren, or the centre's accounts were released to reinstate the full-time staff, this would be their reality. Sometimes, life really did suck.

CHAPTER SEVEN

The following morning, Beth arrived for work ten minutes late. She'd had a rough night, struggling to fall asleep. When she eventually did, her dreams were filled with visions of the night she was attacked. As if that nightmare wasn't bad enough, she dreamt Chloe was also stabbed by Darren. After that, Beth couldn't even contemplate closing her eyes. She had spent the rest of the night rattling around the quiet house, peeping through her curtains and checking her locks. She needed to get a grip on things. *I can't spend the next God-knows-how-many years waiting for him to show up.* She couldn't change what was going to happen, but she could at least try and put it out of her mind until it did. If she carried on the way she was, she would end up driving herself insane. And that wasn't fair to her, or Chloe.

She rushed through the building and rounded the corner toward her office. "Oof." Kathleen's hands gripped her arms, bracing from the collision and preventing Beth from falling. For the second time in three days, she found herself staring up into Kathleen's cool, blue eyes,. The same jolt of arousal flittered through Beth's body.

"Sorry," she mumbled, her voice cracking.

"Not a problem." Kathleen's lips quirked into a smile. "Although, this is becoming a bit of a habit."

Beth felt her cheeks heat, and she took a step back. "Sorry I'm late."

Kathleen's eyebrows raised. "You're the boss, you can be as late as you want."

Beth didn't know about that. It didn't set a very good example to just show up when she wanted. And for Kathleen to suggest that it was okay didn't sit right with her. She was about to reply when she noticed Kathleen's smirk. Beth was overthinking things again. She really did need to get a handle on her life.

An awkward silence surrounded them, and Beth gave in to her need to fill the void. "I managed to speak to my solicitor yesterday. My ex is on tag and probation. As far as I'm aware he doesn't know where I am, so we should be safe, for now."

More silence. Beth watched Kathleen's gaze look everywhere but at her. It was obvious Kathleen didn't want to discuss the situation, and Beth felt like an idiot for bringing it up again. She'd already been rejected after Kathleen saw the scars. Why she thought Kathleen would care now alluded her. She looked toward her office at the end of the hall. "I need to get to work." She didn't give Kathleen a moment to reply but sidestepped her and strode to her office. She would force the awkward encounter from her mind and concentrate on work instead.

Beth couldn't get a read on Kathleen. Yesterday, she was open and caring, even offering a big donation so the fundraiser could go ahead. Today, just the mention of my ex and she closed up. Her posture goes all stiff and her eyes go wide. Beth didn't know what had happened to Kathleen, but something clearly had. There had to be a reason her personality constantly kept changing.

†

Beth grabbed a coffee from the snacks table. *Tonight, will be the first time I'm leading the group instead of being a participant.* It felt strange to her. She was used to listening to others talk and occasionally offering comments. Being the one who initiated the talks was going to be hard. She wasn't a naturally nosy person, preferring the other person to engage with her when they felt ready. Having to lead the night's conversations was going to be difficult.

At the end of her shift, she'd made a quick run to the school to pick up Chloe and drop her off at the sitter's. Chloe wasn't happy about that. She hadn't had a sitter for years. With Darren released, Beth wasn't comfortable leaving Chloe on her own. She still hadn't mentioned her father, and Beth was beginning to worry. One day soon, Beth would need to sit down with her and force a good talk, whether Chloe was ready or not.

Beth wandered over to the stack of chairs and began arranging them into a circle. She had about twenty minutes before everyone would start to arrive, so she used the time to focus on the meeting and not on her ex.

"Hey, Beth."

Beth looked over her shoulder and saw Meredith walking toward her. Beth smiled in return. "Good evening. How was your week?"

Meredith grabbed a chair and helped line them up. "It's been a little busier in the last few days. I'm hoping it'll continue."

"That's good."

They finished with the chairs, and by unspoken communication, headed over to the snacks table. *Now would be the perfect opportunity to talk to Meredith about Kathleen.* Their weird encounter that morning had plagued the back of Beth's mind all day. Meredith was the only one who might know what was going on with her. Beth didn't feel right going behind Kathleen's back but knew trying to talk to Kathleen about it wouldn't get her anywhere. She waited while Meredith fixed herself a coffee and took a sip.

"Can I ask you something about Kathleen?"

Meredith's brows rose, a cautious smile stretching her lips. "Sure."

Beth thought for a moment, trying to find the right way to phrase her question. She couldn't think of a subtle way of asking, so she just blurted out, "Has Kathleen been involved in some kind of trauma?"

"I don't think so. That's a strange question. Why do you ask?"

"On her first day, she walked in on me in the restroom. I had my shirt off, as I had spilled something on it, and she saw my scars. I explained where they came from, and she looked horrified. She didn't speak and just walked out. Yesterday she apologised for her behaviour. But today, when I ran into her again and talked about Darren, she went all weird again. She avoided the conversation, and she looked like she wanted to throw up."

Meredith sighed and looked away. When she looked back, she seemed sad. "As far as I know, nothing has happened to her. From my experience, she isn't very well equipped with dealing with this sort of thing." Meredith said no more, and it was left to Beth to fill in the unspoken words. She gazed at Meredith for a moment and then it clicked.

"She's your ex, isn't she?"

Meredith nodded.

Beth went over to a chair and slumped into it. Over the last few months, she had learned of Meredith's abduction and torture at the hands of a serial killer. She also knew that Meredith had been seeing someone who couldn't deal with the horrific injuries and mood changes. That person had even made Meredith feel as if it was her fault. They had split up not long after Meredith got home.

Meredith sat in the chair next to her, and Beth tilted her head to look at her. "She cheated on you?" she asked, already knowing the answer.

"Yes."

"Christ." Beth shook her head. "Why in the world would you recommend her to work here?" There was no anger in her voice, just confusion. The whole point of the centre was to help abused and vulnerable women. It was clear Kathleen didn't have the emotional capacity for that. Beth didn't want someone here who would make the women feel uncomfortable or less worthy. This was supposed to be a safe place.

"I know it seems like she isn't a good fit, but I promise you, she is a good person. I don't fully know why it was so hard for her when I came home. She said some horrible things. I think she was hurting just as much as I was. She hasn't been dealing with things this past year, and I'm worried about her. I thought if she worked here it might help her heal."

"That's crazy."

"Probably." Meredith smiled. "But please give her a chance. I was with her for four years. We might not have been as close as I would have liked, but we still loved each other."

Beth leaned back into the chair and closed her eyes. Meredith's words didn't help the unease she now felt at having Kathleen there. She prayed Kathleen wouldn't upset any of the women. Beth wouldn't stand for that. She would give Kathleen the benefit of the doubt. However, at the first sign of anything inappropriate, Beth would go to the board and get her sacked. She didn't count the way Kathleen had dismissed her. She could deal with that on her own.

CHAPTER EIGHT

It had been nearly two weeks since Kathleen started at WHCC, and she still felt she was playing catch up. The investigation into the misappropriation of funds was still in full swing, which meant the main accounts were still frozen. The fundraising team had done a great job of doing bucket collections, and the city council had advanced a small portion of next year's budget to help see them through, but they were still way underfunded. Even with Kathleen's knack for numbers, she was still having trouble keeping them in the black.

It wasn't just the stress of running the financial side of things that was causing Kathleen to have sleepless nights. Beth had been on her mind, a lot. Beth had been avoiding her as much as she could, considering they needed to work closely to run the centre. Kathleen couldn't blame her. She hadn't exactly handled Beth's problem with her ex all that well. Every time Kathleen looked at her, the images of the scars on Beth's body came to mind. Kathleen couldn't shake the anxiety that settled in her chest when she thought of the pain Beth must have gone through. Kathleen knew why Beth was avoiding her. She had made her feel ashamed for her injuries. Beth hadn't been alone with her since the day Kathleen froze at the mention of Darren's parole conditions.

Kathleen glanced at the small digital clock on her desk, noting the late hour. Not once in the past two weeks had she been home before nine. She had been given a spare set of keys, so Beth didn't have to stay and wait for her to finish. Kathleen was pleased for that. She didn't think she could cope sitting in silence, trying to work while the tension surrounded them.

She shut down her computer and packed her briefcase. She needed a hot bath and maybe a glass of wine in bed. She switched off the light and headed for the front of the building. As she reached the main reception room, Beth came through the door, her arm around the shoulder of a teenage girl. The girl's clothes were torn, and blood trickled from a small cut on her eyebrow. Kathleen's heart beat wildly, and she gasped. Beth looked up, her eyes going wide at seeing Kathleen.

"Can you find me the first-aid kit?" Beth asked as she strode past with the crying girl. "We'll be up in the night room."

Kathleen watched them go, then glanced toward the front door. It would be so easy to walk away and pretend she hadn't heard the request. Her gaze swung back into the centre proper, after Beth. *What would she think of you if you turn your back on someone in need? You're already way down in her estimation of a decent human being.* She didn't want to lower that opinion any more than it already was. Taking a deep breath, she followed behind.

She grabbed the first-aid kit from the kitchen, then headed up to the night room. She found Beth kneeling in front of the girl, who sat on a low bed. Beth held a cloth to the girl's head, her other hand gently rubbing the girl's thigh. Even from across the room, it wasn't hard to see the compassion in Beth's gaze. Kathleen's heart warmed. She wished she could be that sympathetic, but she knew it was a fruitless dream.

Kathleen put her briefcase down by the door and walked over toward the bed. Beth looked up as she approached, smiling softly, and accepted the first-aid kit Kathleen held out to her.

"Thank you."

"No problem." She took a few steps back, not wanting to intrude on the private moment. The girl looked to be about seventeen. Her blonde hair was tangled and her skin pale. It was obvious she had been in a struggle, and Kathleen's heart clenched at the thought she may have been raped. She bit her lip to stop herself asking questions. It wasn't her place. She glanced over her shoulder at the door.

"You can leave if you want." Beth hadn't even glanced her way.

"It's okay."

Kathleen silently watched Beth clean the cut and apply a small Steri-Strip. She took the girl's hands and whispered something Kathleen couldn't hear. The girl shook her head vigorously, and Beth sighed. She gently cupped the girl's face and smiled, then stood and cleared away the detritus.

The teen lay down, and Beth pulled a blanket over her before heading toward Kathleen.

"Follow me," Beth said.

Kathleen did as asked. They stepped from the room, leaving the door ajar. "Can I ask what happened, or is that confidential?"

Beth shook her head. "No, it's fine. You work here, so it's not betraying confidences." Beth glanced through the doorway at the sleeping girl then back to Kathleen. "Her boyfriend got hopped up on drugs and went crazy, beat her up a little. She's been to the centre before, with a social worker, and had my number. She called and I picked her up."

"Shouldn't she go to the police?"

"I've tried convincing her to, but she won't go. I'll try again in the morning and hopefully persuade her it's the right thing to do."

Kathleen noted the dark circles under Beth's eyes. It was clear she had been having a rough time of it, and all Kathleen wanted to do was make it a little easier for her. She didn't know why. They hardly knew each other, but there was something about Beth that captured her attention.

"Were you planning on staying here?"

"Yes. We don't have the staff at the moment to cover, do we?"

Kathleen detected a hint of anger in Beth's voice, but it wasn't Kathleen's fault other employees had stolen from the charity. She was working her ass off to try and make the funds they had cover their needs. She refrained from commenting, knowing Beth was under a lot of stress. She glanced at the sleeping girl, words falling from her lips before she could stop them.

"I can stay with her if you like, so you can go home."

"Why would you do that?" Beth brow knitted in a frown.

Kathleen shrugged and rubbed the back of her neck, not sure why she had offered. She looked at Beth again, and the answer was obvious. "I don't have anyone or anything waiting at home for me. You do. You should go and rest. I'll stay." Beth was silent for a moment, just staring at Kathleen like she had grown two heads. She struggled not to fidget under the scrutiny.

"Are you sure?" Beth asked carefully, scepticism in her features.

"Yeah."

Beth glanced once again at the girl. "Okay. But call me if you need anything or if there is a problem."

"I will."

"Okay."

Beth briefly touched Kathleen's forearm, and Kathleen felt the warmth even through her suit jacket. She hadn't thought a simple touch could make her heart flutter, but it did. What was it about Beth that had Kathleen feeling the most human she had felt in months?

She watched Beth walk away, then went back into the night room, her bath and wine forgotten. She would look over some paperwork, then try and sleep on the not-so-comfortable looking bed. She hoped the teen wouldn't wake up, because Kathleen knew, without a doubt, she wouldn't be able to handle talking to her. She hadn't been around that many youngsters, especially ones who had been beaten up. The thought of comforting her terrified her.

†

Kathleen slowly came to awareness but didn't open her eyes. She had a feeling she was being watched. Ignoring the cramp in her side, she turned her head to the left and glanced at the camp bed ten feet away. The girl was sitting up, chin in her hands, looking at Kathleen through narrowed eyelids. Kathleen didn't know the time, but she guessed it was about seven in the morning. She swung her legs over the edge and sat up, running her hands through her hair.

"Morning," Kathleen said, her voice rough with sleep.

"Where's Beth?"

"She went home last night. She'll be back in a little while." The girl looked toward the door, and Kathleen recognised the panic in her gaze. She herself had wanted to bolt last night. She knew Beth wouldn't be pleased if the teen wasn't there when she arrived. "What's your name?"

"Teegan."

"You can call me Kath."

"Thank you for staying." Teegan smiled, then blushed, touching the bandage on her head.

Kathleen shrugged. "No problem. You hungry?" Teegan nodded vigorously. "Come on then." She stood from the bed and stretched her back muscles, instantly missing her king-size mattress at home. Teegan followed her to the kitchen. Kathleen wasn't much of a cook, but she could make toast and maybe fry an egg. No words were spoken as they set about collecting plates, bread, butter, and jam. Kathleen made the toast, and Teegan made coffee. A few minutes later, they were seated opposite each other at one of the tables.

Kathleen racked her brain for a topic of conversation to fill the empty void. "Does it hurt?" She indicated the cut on Teegan's head. Teegan shrugged.

"Not really. I've had worse."

Kathleen sucked in a breath, not sure how to respond. She hated to think of any more violence happening to such a young girl. "Do you need to call your mum or anyone?"

"I live with Shane, my boyfriend. Parents are dead."

It keeps getting worse! Kathleen was at a loss. Teegan was so young and had obviously been through a lot. If she was on her own, it was no wonder she stayed with a boyfriend who took drugs and beat her. She probably didn't have any other options.

"Shane hasn't always been like this. We met in school, and he was really sweet, despite his folks being assholes. He made me feel like a princess. When he hit sixteen, he started hanging around with some dicks from college and began smoking crack. He can't get off it, and I don't know how to help him." Her eyes dimmed. "I'm not even sure he wants to quit."

"What happened to your parents?"

"Car crash. Shane said I could stay with him and his family, then about six months ago, we moved into a bedsit. It's become more like a crack den. People coming and going all day and night. I hate it."

Teegan's eyes teared, and it broke Kathleen's heart. "Why don't you leave?"

"I have nowhere else to go." She shrugged again and bit into her toast.

Kathleen didn't know a lot about social services and the like, but surely there was someone out there who could help. "Have you tried—"

"Please don't go into social-worker mode. I've had enough of people telling me what to do."

"I wasn't doing that. I just thought...never mind." Kathleen took a swig of coffee to help disguise her inability to say the right thing. What did she think she was going to achieve? Teegan had obviously been through all this before and didn't need Kathleen trying to help. For seventeen years old, she had seen a lot in her short life. The silence stretched between them again. Kathleen forced more toast down and tried to find a safer topic that wouldn't make things more awkward.

"What kind of music do you like?" Teegan glanced up, and Kathleen could see the relief in her face at the cessation of talking about her problems. Teegan smiled and pulled her mobile from her jeans pocket. She scrolled for a moment, then fast-paced drum and bass started playing. To Kathleen, it sounded like noise. Teegan apparently loved it, as she started tapping the table in time to the drums. Before long, Kathleen joined in, trying to match the rhythm. She was useless, and Teegan laughed at her attempts. Kathleen was pleased she could help the youngster take her mind off her ordeal.

†

Beth unlocked the main door to the centre and flipped on the lights. She had worried all night about leaving Teegan with Kathleen, not wanting Kathleen to make the teen feel uncomfortable. It wasn't that she didn't trust her. She did, but she knew from Meredith and her own experience that Kathleen didn't like dealing with trauma. Teegan had been through a lot in the past two years, and Beth didn't want Kathleen to add to her low self-esteem. Beth could have stayed, but she wasn't happy about leaving Chloe with the sitter overnight. Chloe wasn't happy either about being dropped off when the call from Teegan had come in. She did understand Beth didn't have a choice but was ecstatic when Beth called to say she was collecting her to go home.

Beth walked through the main room, intent on heading upstairs. At half seven in the morning, Teegan and Kathleen would probably still be asleep. A faint noise drew her in the direction of the dining room. As she got closer to the door, she could hear laughter and the sounds of heavy metal playing. Beth peeped through the glass of the door. What she saw amused her. Kathleen and Teegan were jumping up and down, bobbing their heads to the beat. Teegan's smile was wide, and her skin was flushed. Beth looked at Kathleen, and her breath caught in her throat. Even jumping around like a crazy person, she was beautiful. Her thick blonde hair flowed around her face and shoulders, and her hips captivated Beth's attention as they swayed in erotic circles. Beth couldn't deny the physical attraction. Her decision to leave Darren, because she thought she was a lesbian, turned out to be the right one. She had always had an awareness of women but thought it was just admiration. It wasn't until she met Jude that she realised her admiration was in fact attraction. Nothing happened between them, but the encounter was enough to make Beth want to make the biggest decision in her life, one that had nearly ended it.

She pushed open the door and cleared her throat loudly. Immediately, they stopped dancing and looked toward her. Kathleen's face went a deep red, her chest rising and falling quickly as she tried to catch her breath.

"Hey, Beth. Want to join in?" Teegan asked.

Beth smiled. "No, thank you. My dancing days are over."
Teegan turned the music off, and Beth grinned at Kathleen.
"Didn't know you were such a rocker."

Kathleen's blush deepened. "It's not my usual music, but
I might have been converted. It's quite the workout."

The way she said workout evoked images Beth didn't
need in her head. She felt her own cheeks heat under
Kathleen's intense gaze. Beth looked away, back at Teegan.
"Are you okay to chat?" The joy left Teegan's eyes and she
nodded. "Head into my office, and I'll be there in a minute."
She handed Teegan the key to her door.

"Thanks Kathleen, for everything," Teegan said.

"No problem. Come by anytime if you fancy learning
about proper music."

Teegan laughed then left them alone.

"I take it everything went okay last night," Beth probed.

"Yeah. It was a bit awkward when we woke up, but as
you can see, we soon sorted that out."

"Thank you for staying. I appreciate it."

"It's fine." Kathleen's smile disappeared as she turned
serious. "I don't know how you do it, looking after all these
women and children."

Beth shrugged; unsure what Kathleen meant. "I don't
really think about it."

"You all do amazing work here." Kathleen paused for a
moment. Her forehead creased as she seemed to stare off into
the distance. "I wish I could be like you."

The quietly spoken words floored Beth. She wasn't
anything special, she just did her job. Yeah, a certain amount
of caring about people had to be involved, but she just did
what needed to be done. As she gazed at Kathleen's
expression, she realised Meredith was right. Kathleen did

have a good heart, and it was clear to Beth how lost Kathleen was. She took a step forward and lightly touched her arm.

"You don't need to be like me, Kath, just be you."

"I suck at this."

Beth smiled at the choice of words. Apparently, Teegan's favourite saying had rubbed off. "You don't suck. Look how you handled Teegan this morning. I haven't seen her that happy in a long time."

Kathleen shook her head. "I don't know about that. I tried to talk to her about what happened, but she shot me down."

"Teegan isn't one to trust easily. It takes time. Just be her friend; that's what she needs."

Kathleen nodded, but her consternation remained. "I want to know what happened last night, but I don't think I should ask you. It wouldn't be fair to betray her confidences."

"See, you do know how to do this."

Beth was pleased when Kathleen smiled widely. Obviously, that was the right thing to say. "I need to go talk to her. Are you going home now?"

"No, I'll clean myself up and head to my office. I slept long enough, so I'm not tired."

"Okay. Do you have time later to discuss the fundraiser?"

"Yeah, just come find me."

"All right. I'll see you later then."

"Yes."

They stared at each other for a few long moments, and Beth was lost in her gaze. It could be her imagination, but she swore she saw a flicker of attraction in Kathleen's eyes. *That's crazy.* Kathleen had never given her any indication she was interested. They spent most of their time avoiding each other. Still, there was something in that intense gaze.

Beth closed her eyes and turned away, needing to get her head out of the clouds and back to her job. She didn't have time for all this nonsense. Without another word, she walked out of the room in the direction of her office, Kathleen's blue eyes plaguing her thoughts.

CHAPTER NINE

Three o'clock that afternoon Beth headed across the corridor. Her stomach twisted with nerves at the prospect of seeing Kathleen for the first time since early that morning. After spending forty minutes with Teegan, Beth helped Francine prepare sandwiches for the clients and set up the day room for the jobs fair that took place at eleven. She'd had a busy day so far, with no time to examine her reaction to Kathleen. Beth was confused by her own feelings. She knew she was physically attracted to Kathleen. Who wouldn't be? Kathleen was tall, with thick blonde hair and a trim body. Beth was mesmerised by the shadows in Kathleen's eyes, and for some unknown reason, wanted to get to know her better. A week ago, she would have thought that notion stupid. Kathleen's rudeness had put Beth off, but seeing her dancing and laughing with Teegan had changed her perspective. There was more to Kathleen than Beth realised, and she wanted to find out all she could about the complicated woman.

She stopped outside the closed door and knocked twice, entering when Kathleen called from the inside. Her heartbeat tripped when Kathleen looked up and smiled at her.

"Is now a good time to talk?" Beth's voice came out steady and clear, which was amazing. Her nerves had just doubled.

"Of course. Take a seat." Kathleen closed the program on her computer, then folded her hands on the desk and gave Beth her full attention. "How was Teegan when she left?"

The question threw Beth for a second, not expecting Kathleen to ask. "She's okay. Shane was constantly ringing and texting. You could say he was worried about her, but I think he just wanted to find out if she went to the police."

"I want to kill him for hurting her." Kathleen's eyes darkened.

"Me too, but she's old enough to make her own choices. She's been to social services before, but she ran away from the foster home. She'll be eighteen in a few months, then there will be nothing anyone can do, unless she asks for help."

Kathleen looked away for a long moment. Beth could see her trying to calm herself, biting her lip while taking deep breaths. Observing the keen response stirred Beth's affection for Kathleen. Maybe Meredith was right, and this was the best place for Kathleen to find herself.

"How are the plans for the fundraiser coming along?" Kathleen asked.

"Thanks to your donation, we can go ahead with our original idea. We want to do a winter ball. Hire out a hall and have a band and maybe an auction. When the alcohol is flowing, people are more willing to spend and donate."

Kathleen nodded. "That's a good idea. Will there be food?"

"Yeah. Francine will do finger food for the guests."

"I can give you some more money, and we can get proper catering."

"No. Francine is more than capable of putting together a spread. She does all our events, and we've never had any complaints."

"I'm just suggesting maybe a better class of food—"

"We're supposed to be doing a charity event, not some fancy gala or something. We can't just throw money at it. Donors will assume that if we can afford high-quality food and drinks we don't need their money."

Kathleen scrunched her face in obvious concentration. "I suppose that's true."

Beth could tell she wasn't happy with her offer being turned down. "Trust me, I know what I'm doing." *And when you're no longer around to just hand out money, we'd need to revert to our original way of working things.* It was best to keep it as is. "You've already done enough by donating the funds to put on the event. If you hadn't, we might not have been able to even do this year's fundraiser. So, thank you."

Kathleen blushed and cleared her throat. "What about alcohol?"

"We still have a lot of bottles that have been donated over time, as well as some things for an auction. The fundraising team will spend the next couple of months hitting up local businesses to see what they can donate for prizes. Then we send out the invitations."

"I can call some of my contacts and extend invitations to them. They're all loaded and love a chance to do a tax write-off."

Beth knew that businesses were allowed to offset some of their tax liability with charitable donations. She didn't necessarily agree with them giving just for a tax break but knew centres like WHCC couldn't run on government funding alone.

"That'll be great. The more people the better."

They gazed at each other for a moment, and Beth felt her skin flush. She was beginning to realise that blushing was something she wouldn't be able to control around Kathleen.

Kathleen cleared her throat and said, "Listen, I was wondering if—" Her ringing phone cut her off. She smiled apologetically. "Sorry."

"No problem. I'll see you later." Beth stood from the chair and left as quickly as she could, her heart hammering in her chest. For a moment, she'd thought Kathleen was about to ask her out. *That's crazy.* Kathleen would probably assume she was straight, what with an ex-husband and all. Thinking Kathleen had any interest in her at all was ridiculous. No, this was a one-way crush on Beth's part, and it needed to stop.

†

Kathleen rounded the corner of the building, then entered the small carpark. A hectic day on top of staying the night with Teegan had Kathleen ready to drop. It didn't help that images of Beth's soulful, brown eyes kept interrupting her thoughts. She was beginning to accept she had feelings for Beth that went beyond the professional. They'd only known each other a few weeks, but every time Beth popped into her head, Kathleen's heart raced. Beth was so caring and compassionate with the women at the centre, and it made Kathleen want Beth to be that way with her. She had always been self-sufficient. Never in her life had she wanted someone to take care of her. Beth brought out a need Kathleen didn't know she could ever feel. For a few brief moments, after they'd talked about Teegan, Kathleen had wanted to confess all, to tell her secret wishes that Beth could somehow make it all right. It was a stupid thought, and Kathleen had quickly quashed the idea. Beth didn't need Kathleen adding to her problems.

As if thinking of her infatuation made her appear, Kathleen caught sight of Beth across the carpark. The bonnet was up on her car, and she was leaning over the engine bay. Kathleen could hear cursing. She took a breath and walked over to her.

"Something wrong?" She peered over Beth's shoulder at the engine. The faint whiff of Beth's perfume set off a hum of arousal low in her belly. She swallowed hard. Beth jerked at the sound of her voice, causing Kathleen to stumble back a step. Beth spun around with her hand on her chest, breathing hard.

"Jesus, you scared me."

"Sorry." Kathleen looked away from Beth, not quite getting a handle on her reaction to Beth's lovely features. She glanced again at the car. "What's the problem?"

"Damn thing won't start. I've called my mechanic, but he's out of town and can't get here until tomorrow."

"So, you thought you'd fix it yourself?" Kathleen smirked at the consternation on Beth's face.

"I'll have you know I'm quite good with my hands."

The smirk grew into a wide grin and a wink that caused Beth to blush furiously. "Good to know." Why she thought flirting with Beth was a good idea, Kathleen didn't know. She rested her hand on the car. "Can I give you a ride?" Beth stared at her, her eyes wide and blush deepening. Kathleen realised how that sounded. "Oh, God." She covered her face with her hands to hide her own blush and shook her head. "I meant, can I give you a lift?" Beth's lilting laughter caught her attention, and she mentally added another thing she found fascinating about her.

"Are you sure?" Beth glanced back at her car.

"Of course. Come on." Without waiting for Beth to respond, Kathleen walked toward her own car. She didn't relish the idea of them sitting so close together, but evidently, she was a glutton for punishment.

She got in the driver's seat and waited for Beth to join her. Conversation was sparse, as Beth gave directions to her house. Thirty minutes later, Kathleen pulled up outside a small bungalow. The front garden was bare; just a small hedge lined the boundary. No plants or shrubs, just neatly trimmed grass covering the ground. Nothing adorned the outside walls and the blinds were closed over the windows. The scene struck Kathleen as odd. She shifted in her seat to look at Beth, noting her gaze frantically searching the immediate area. Kathleen drew her brows down. *What? Oh.* Beth's ex-husband was free. Kathleen laid a reassuring hand on Beth's thigh, causing Beth to start.

"Do you want me to walk you in?"

Beth blinked rapidly as if clearing her fear away. "No, it's okay."

She made no attempt to exit the car. Kathleen could only imagine the terror Beth must be feeling. She wondered if Beth was like this every time she came home from work. She hated the thought of her struggling so much. She sighed and shook her head. She unclipped her seatbelt and opened her door. She walked around to Beth's side and opened her door. "Come on." Beth stared at her for a moment, then nodded. She unclipped her own seat belt and stepped out. She led Kathleen up the short walk, unlocked the front door and went inside. Kathleen shut the door behind her and glanced around the room. The inside wasn't much better than the outside. The lounge was cramped, even though furnished with only the essentials: couch, tv, and coffee table. The decor was...beige. To Kathleen's mind, the banal interior looked like a rented property which hadn't yet been decorated to the renter's taste.

Beth must have noticed her staring. "It's easier to leave quickly if you don't have much stuff to take with you."

She said no more and strode to what Kathleen assumed was the kitchen. She debated whether to follow or not, then realised her previous desire to flee when faced with Beth's past was absent. All she wanted to do was take away the pain that was clear in Beth's eyes. She took a deep breath and followed.

Beth stood at the kitchen sink, staring at the blank canvas of the window blind. Kathleen wondered what the view was like behind the obstruction, hating that Beth didn't feel safe enough in her own home to enjoy the simple pleasure of watching nature. She was about to speak when Beth turned quickly to face her, unshed tears in her eyes.

"Now he's out, I don't think I'll ever be free of him." She folded her arms around herself. "What kind of life is this for Chloe?" She motioned to the sparse home.

Kathleen had no words of comfort to offer. Her own failings made it hard to find the right thing to say, so she stayed quiet. She couldn't bear the look of pain in Beth's eyes. "Come here." She stepped forward and held out her arms. After a moment of hesitation, Beth stepped into Kathleen's space, wrapping her arms around her waist. Kathleen cradled her head under her chin and wrapped her other arm around her shoulder. Beth squeezed her tighter, and Kathleen felt tears on her skin. Beth's body shook as she cried, and Kathleen held her closer still. She felt strange offering comfort, but she found she didn't want to move, not until she knew Beth would be all right. As much as she thought she couldn't handle any type of crisis, she knew deep down, she would do anything to help Beth. Kathleen hated the man who was putting Beth through this. She didn't deserve to live her life like a prisoner. They remained wrapped up in each other for a few minutes. Kathleen was loath to let her go, but eventually Beth pulled away, scrubbing her hand over her face.

"Sorry," Beth said.

"No, don't apologise." Kathleen reached up and gently brushed away the remaining tears on her cheek. She gazed into Beth's eyes and something shifted inside her. Her body trembled. She realised she had never felt this protective of anyone before, not even Meredith. She dropped her hand and looked away, not willing to put a name to the feelings she had toward Beth. "Where's Chloe?" she asked, trying to break the tension.

"She's at the sitter's. She doesn't really need to be looked after, but with Darren..." She didn't finish the sentence. "She'll be home soon."

Kathleen needed to get out of there, to spend some time figuring out her emotions. She glanced back at Beth. "Do you want to order pizza for dinner? I'd love to meet her."

"You sure?" Beth's face matched her incredulous tone.

Kathleen shrugged. "Yeah, why not?" Kathleen wasn't really a kid person, but she was curious to meet the younger version of Beth. And if she was honest, she wasn't ready to leave just yet.

CHAPTER TEN

Kathleen sat at Beth's small kitchen table sipping coffee. She would have preferred a glass of wine, but Beth hadn't offered. It would have been rude to ask. They hadn't spoken a word in the last twenty minutes, and Kathleen knew that Beth was trying to collect herself from her earlier breakdown. The quiet was fine with Kathleen. She didn't know what to say anyway. She watched Beth putter about the kitchen, tidying up non-existent messes and wiping down the counter tops. Her movements were shaky. Beth's turmoil made Kathleen's chest hurt.

"Are you okay?"

Beth stilled, her back to Kathleen, and her shoulders slumped. She shook her head. "No." She turned and smiled. "But I will be."

The smile was fake, and all Kathleen wanted to do was to take Beth in her arms again. Holding her had felt so right. They fit well together, but unless Beth initiated the contact, Kathleen would keep her hands to herself.

The front door opened, and Kathleen turned her head. A young girl came up the hallway, then turned into another room. Kathleen assumed that was her bedroom.

"Excuse me a moment." Beth threw her cloth into the sink and went after her daughter.

Kathleen tried not to listen, but it wasn't hard to hear the raised voices coming from the other room. A moment later, Beth re-entered the kitchen and shut the door. She slumped into a seat opposite Kathleen and rested her head in her hands. Kathleen kept quiet, allowing Beth to tell her what happened if she wanted to, or not.

"Chloe isn't hungry." Beth lowered her hands, gazing at Kathleen. "She hates that I make her go to the sitter, but it's for her own safety. I can't have her here alone if her father decides to turn up."

"Do you think he will?"

Beth seemed to search for an answer on the kitchen wall. She nodded. "Yeah, I do. I don't think he's done with me yet."

The quietly spoken words sent a chill over Kathleen, and she shivered from the knowledge the ex might still want to kill Beth. She wanted to know what had happened five years ago to make him snap like that, but she didn't know how to ask.

"Do you want to know what happened?" Beth asked, surprising Kathleen.

"Only if you want to tell me."

"You won't get all weird on me and make me feel like crap?"

Kathleen sucked in a breath. She knew she had done the exact same thing twice before. Beth had every right to call her out on her behaviour, but she hadn't expected her to be so direct.

"I'm sorry, these things are hard for me to deal with, but I want to know what he did to you, and why." She reached across the small table and entwined their fingers, showing Beth she wasn't going anywhere. Beth stared at her for a long while. Kathleen made sure to keep eye contact under the weight of the assessment. She tried to convey her full support. Beth gave a quick nod and took a breath, and Kathleen steeled herself for what would likely be a horrendous story.

"My marriage to Darren had always been strained. He was controlling and moody a lot of the time. He didn't like me going places without him and would constantly call me at work. I didn't notice at first — I thought I was in love. Over time, things got worse. Once I had Chloe, I gave up working and things settled down. He was happy when I was at home all day, and he no longer got angry over stupid stuff.

"Eventually, I went back to work. I met someone who made me question things about myself." Beth paused, narrowing her eyes slightly as if wondering whether to continue. Kathleen squeezed her hands.

"Please, go on."

"Her name was Jude. I found myself developing feelings for her. Nothing happened between us, but I realised my feelings for her were more than I'd ever felt for Darren. Over the next few months, I questioned a lot of things and finally accepted I was a lesbian. It wasn't just Jude I had a crush on.

All throughout my life, I had an awareness of women. Jude just confirmed what I had buried deeply.

"Five years ago, I asked Darren for a divorce. I made the mistake of telling him the real reason why." Beth's eyes teared, and she stared down at the table. Kathleen didn't say anything, just continued to hold her hands.

The next part of the story would be the attack. Kathleen wasn't sure she wanted to hear it, but she had made a promise. She wouldn't make Beth feel bad for what had happened to her. She had made that mistake before, and with Meredith. She wouldn't do it again. She scooted her chair closer to Beth and squeezed her thigh, while holding her other hand.

"It's okay," she said. "I'm here."

Beth nodded. "He glared at me, like an angry, stone statue. Then he exploded and charged at me. He wrapped his hands around my throat, lifting me off the floor. He threw me across the room, then disappeared. I was barely conscious. When he returned, he had a knife gripped in his hand. He said the only way I would ever leave him was in a box. I tried to crawl away, but he stabbed me in the back. He turned me and plunged the knife into my chest." Beth lifted her hand and touched the place where Kathleen remembered seeing that awful scar. "I think he thought I was dead when he left. I lay there all night, until Chloe came home the next day."

"She found you?" *God, how horrible was that?* Kathleen couldn't imagine how Chloe coped with finding her mother stabbed and bleeding. The girl would have been under ten years old. "I'm so sorry."

Beth smiled sadly. "It's okay."

"No, it's not. And they've let him out?"

"Yeah. Apparently, he's a changed man, a model prisoner." Beth's gaze lowered, and she took a shuddering breath. "If he finds out where I am, he'll kill me."

Kathleen gathered Beth close as she cried. "I won't let that happen," she whispered fiercely. How she thought she would be able to stop him she didn't know, but she did know she wouldn't let Beth face this alone. "Do you think he knows where you are?"

Beth pulled back and shrugged. "I moved from up north and changed our names. If he really wanted to find us, he could. I just really hope he doesn't."

They were interrupted by the kitchen door opening. A sullen-looking Chloe entered. Kathleen dropped her arms from around Beth, who stood and hugged her daughter.

"I'm sorry, Mum."

"It's okay, sweetheart." She smoothed her hand over Chloe's blonde hair. "Do you want that pizza now?" Chloe nodded, and Beth asked Kathleen, "Still want to stick around for dinner?"

The question was innocuous enough, but Kathleen read the subtext. Beth was asking if her story had scared her off. Would she flee like she always had? "Find me a menu." Kathleen grinned.

†

Beth took another bite of pizza and studied Kathleen as she chatted with Chloe across the table from her. She hadn't thought she would ever tell Kathleen about Darren, not with the way Kathleen always wigged out on her. She had been surprised, though, when the words came out and Kathleen had sat there listening, giving her full attention. It had been good to let it out and to acknowledge the fear she felt from Darren coming back into her life. She prayed he wouldn't, but she wasn't naive. This wasn't over. She just hoped that, when he came for her, Chloe wouldn't be around. She no longer felt safe in her own home. Maybe it was time to think about moving again. Her gaze slid to Chloe. It wouldn't be fair to her to move schools, away from her friends, but she would have to learn to live with it. Chloe's safety was paramount. If she ended up hating Beth, it would be worth it to know she was safe. Her musings were interrupted by Chloe's voice.

"Mum, can I go to my room?"

"Of course." She watched, as Chloe said good night to Kathleen, then left them alone in the kitchen. Beth had been surprised how well Kathleen and Chloe got along. They talked for ages about Chloe's schoolwork and her plans to be a veterinarian. Beth had gotten the impression that Kathleen wasn't a people person, but both Chloe and Teegan had connected with her. *So have I.* Her presence in the house made Beth feel not so alone. She realised she was staring, when Kathleen cleared her throat.

"Your daughter is really nice."

"Thank you. I'm amazed she's turned out so well, considering. I fear that it's all going to come out in an unhealthy way, and she'll end up doing drugs or something."

"Just keep doing what you're doing. She'll be fine."

Beth knew they were empty words said to make her feel better. No one knew what the future would bring, and she was under no illusion that finding her mum near death in a pool of blood hadn't affected Chloe. There was no need to point that out to Kathleen, she wasn't stupid.

"Do you want to stay for a drink?" She wasn't quite ready for Kathleen to leave. It wasn't just not wanting to be on her own. She also wanted to find out more about her.

"Wine would be nice, if you have it."

Beth nodded and stood, clearing the pizza box away. She reached for two glasses and the bottle of red in an upper cabinet. "Let's go to the lounge." She led Kathleen to the sofa, then poured them each a glass. They settled at each end, turned toward each other, and sipped in the quiet. Beth's curiosity got the better of her. "Tell me about yourself."

"Not much to tell, I'm afraid." Kathleen looked away, her forehead creasing.

"I find that hard to believe." The shadows in her eyes were proof of hidden depths and layers, and Beth wanted to know what caused her to look so haunted. "You're Meredith's ex, aren't you?"

Kathleen's hand trembled, as she lifted her glass to take a drink. "How do you know that?"

"I was speaking to her not long ago and I guessed." Beth could tell she had hit a raw nerve. The look of panic on Kathleen's features wasn't hard to miss. She reached out her hand and touched Kathleen's knee. "It's okay, you don't have to tell me."

"I'm not a very good person, Beth. Throughout my adult life, I only cared about business. There wasn't a deal I couldn't close, a client I couldn't schmooze. I was the best at what I did, and nothing else mattered." She sighed and shook her head. After a large gulp of wine, she put the empty glass on the carpet. "I met Meredith at an event, and we hit it off. I thought she was just another prize for me to win." She smiled sadly. "She won my heart though. We dated for a long time, but we were never really together, you know. I never fully opened myself up to her. I was too busy working and trying to impress everyone."

"You loved her though, didn't you?"

"Yeah, just not as much as I should." Kathleen stood from the sofa and paced the small lounge, shoving her hands into her trouser pockets. "When she was taken, I was obviously devastated. After a couple of months, we assumed she was dead, and I just went back to work. I earned more money in the eight months she was gone than I ever had before. I guess I was just ignoring it all."

She settled back down next to Beth and didn't speak for a moment, her gaze focused in the past. When she turned with wounded eyes, it took all of Beth's willpower not to collect and hold her in her arms.

"Tell me," Beth said softly.

"When she came back, I couldn't cope with what that bastard had done to her. She was covered in scars, and she wasn't the same high-flying estate agent I knew. I distanced myself from her, said some really nasty things, and cheated on her." Kathleen buried her head in her hands, her shoulders shaking. When she'd composed herself enough to lift her head again, her cheeks were wet with tears. Beth's heart cracked from the raw pain in Kathleen's eyes. "How could I do that to her, after all she had been through?"

"I can't imagine it was a picnic for you either."

"But I only cared about myself." She slumped back into the cushion. Her hands lay limp on her thighs. "We broke up, and since that night I have hated myself. My work began to suffer, and I no longer cared about myself. Eventually, my boss told me to take some leave and sort myself out."

"Are you worried he won't take you back?"

Kathleen shook her head. "No. I've made Gerard millions over the years. I'm the best broker he has. He knows I'm too valuable to the company."

Beth didn't think Kathleen was bragging. She knew from Kathleen's work at the centre just how talented she was with numbers. Beth didn't like how she had treated Meredith, but it was apparent that she felt tremendous guilt over her actions. Looking at her now, she could see the stress Kathleen was feeling over all of it. A moment of hesitation flittered through Beth's mind over her attraction to her. *If she could treat Meredith that way after being with her for years, how can I think she would treat me any differently?* Earlier, in the kitchen, Kathleen had stayed engaged and listened, while Beth told of her own experience with Darren. Perhaps Kathleen had changed.

"Are you still in love with her?" Kathleen rolled her head to the side, roaming over Beth's face with a gaze so intense Beth blushed under the perusal.

"No," Kathleen whispered.

They stared at each other for moment, and Beth knew Kathleen was feeling the attraction too. It would only take a small movement on Beth's part to bring their faces closer together and kiss her. Fear held her back. She wasn't in the mood to get her heart broken.

"It's getting late. I should go." Kathleen seemed to understand Beth's hesitancy. "I'll come by in the morning and pick you both up."

"You don't need to do that. I can get a taxi."

"Nonsense. I want to."

They continued to gaze at each other, and words left Beth's mouth before she could stop them. "Why don't you stay here for the night? It's silly to drive home just to come back again in a few hours."

Kathleen grinned. "I'm a little old to be sleeping on sofas."

"You can have my bed, and I'll share with Chloe."

"Won't she mind?"

"Probably. But she has other things to be pissed at me about. That'll just be one more thing to add to the list."

"Okay, thank you."

Beth broke eye contact and poured them both another glass of wine. She checked in on Chloe to make sure she was settled, then headed back into the lounge. It had been an emotional evening for both women, and she was done with talking for now. She settled back on the couch and suggested they watched a comedy, which Kathleen agreed to. They found something on Netflix and spent the next ninety minutes laughing and sipping wine. Eventually, the film finished, and she showed Kathleen to her room. She gave her a spare set of pyjamas and a toothbrush. After she'd said good night, thoughts of Kathleen stretched out in her bed were making her body heat.

†

Kathleen lay on her back in the dark, staring up at the ceiling. She took a deep breath through her nose, inhaling the fresh scent of Beth's sheets and the unique smell that was completely Beth. *How on earth did I end up staying in her bed?* Kathleen had no intention of spending the night. She'd just wanted to give Beth a lift home and be on her way. As much as she wanted to distance herself from Beth, she just couldn't do it. Kathleen was finding herself inexplicably

91

drawn to her. The physical attraction she felt for her was understandable. Beth was beautiful. It was the emotional attraction that had Kathleen worried. She found a deep need to protect Beth, to comfort her. That thought made her stomach knot painfully. Her treatment of Meredith should be ringing alarm bells in her head. She had no right to get attached to Beth. *I'll end up hurting her the same way I did Meredith.* She just couldn't find the strength to walk away. *Perhaps I am changing.* She shook her head at her musings. She couldn't change. She was a bitch. Soon enough, Beth would realise that, if she hadn't already. Telling Beth about Meredith should have put an end to any attraction Beth might be feeling. *I know she's interested.* She could see it in her eyes and the blush that tinted her skin. Kathleen let her mind wander, as she thought about what it would be like to make love to Beth. They fit together well. She knew that from holding her. Just the feel of Beth in her arms sent Kathleen's heart racing. She imagined peeling her clothes off and kissing her skin, settling her weight on top of her as she caressed her. Kathleen's hand began to stroke her own stomach under the top she wore, the stirrings of arousal flooding her system. As she imagined kissing her way down Beth's throat, her eyes flew open and her hand stilled. She could clearly see the scar above Beth's heart. Beth had come so close to death. Kathleen shuddered at the thought.

A noise from the kitchen startled her, and she strained her ear to listen. Feeling an irresistible pull toward Beth, Kathleen got out of bed and crept out of the room. She peered through the darkness into the kitchen. Light from the fridge illuminated the scene, as Beth drank from a milk carton. She must have sensed a presence, because her head turned, and she locked gazes with Kathleen. Having been caught staring, Kathleen made her way into the kitchen. Beth closed the fridge door, leaving them bathed in the moonlight that seeped through the window blind.

"Are you okay?" Kathleen whispered.

Beth held up her phone. "I had a call, but when I answered no one was there. I thought it might have been someone needing the centre, but the line went dead."

Beth's gaze travelled down Kathleen's body slowly, and Kathleen couldn't help her skin heating from the frank examination. They were on dangerous ground. The setting was too intimate, the pull between them too great. Kathleen's breath caught, as Beth put her phone on the table and took a step closer. The fingers she was running up Kathleen's bare arm were sending shivers throughout her body.

"What are you doing?" Kathleen's whisper came out strangled.

"I don't know," Beth replied, as she rose on tiptoes and kissed Kathleen on the underside of her jaw. "But I need to know what it's like to kiss you."

Beth kissed her again, closer to her lips, and Kathleen closed her eyes, thrilling at the warm lips that gently caressed her skin. She knew she should stop this, knew it was a mistake, but her resolve slipped. She gave in to what she had been wishing for since she'd first met Beth. She quashed the urge to throw Beth on to the table, to take her hard and fast. She gently cradled Beth's face in her trembling hands and brought her mouth to Beth's. The first touch of lips nearly crushed her with the exquisite feel of Beth pressed against her. Kathleen pulled back slightly, making eye contact with Beth in the near darkness surrounding them. What she saw made her forget to breathe. She brought Beth's mouth back to hers and kissed her with a passion she didn't know she possessed. She opened her lips and drew Beth in to her. The kiss turned urgent. Beth's arms wrapped around her neck and held Kathleen firmly in place. Kathleen backed her up against the nearest wall, inserting a thigh between her legs, which parted greedily for her. Beth groaned into her mouth.

Kathleen had never felt anything like this before, not even with Meredith. Her need was overwhelming. The little voice in her head made itself known, telling her she should stop this now before it went too far. Beth wasn't in a good place emotionally. *She'll likely regret this in the morning.* Using what little willpower she had left, she grasped Beth's waist and held her in place. Kathleen stepped back a few inches, so their bodies no longer touched. She rested her forehead on Beth's shoulder, both of them breathing heavily.

"We shouldn't be doing this," Kathleen mumbled into Beth's T-shirt, her hands twitching where they touched bare skin on Beth's waist.

Beth untangled her hand from Kathleen's hair and skimmed down her throat to rest above her heart. "I couldn't help myself. I'm sorry."

"Please, don't apologise." Kathleen lifted her head to see Beth's eyes. She grinned. "I rather enjoyed myself." Her grin faded. "But we can't do this." She took another step back, completely disentangling herself from Beth. "As much as I want to, neither of us is in a great place right now. I don't want to have any regrets. Not with you." Just the very thought of hurting Beth made her heart ache in a way she never thought possible.

Beth straightened her T-shirt and ran her hands through her hair, her gaze locked on the floor. Finally, she looked up. "I know you're right, but there is something about you that I can't defend myself from." She pulled out a chair and sat down heavily, resting her head in her hand. She gazed up at Kathleen. "I've tried to tell myself that it's a bad idea, that we're not a good match, but I can't get you out of here,"— she tapped her head — "or here," then her heart.

Kathleen closed her eyes. Beth's words thrilled her, but she knew them to be false emotions. How could Beth ever be attracted to her? She had no doubt that the problems Beth faced with Darren were putting her rational thought out of whack. As soon as she had resolved things regarding Darren, Beth would be mortified about what had just happened between them. Kathleen needed to put a stop to this before it got even more out of hand. She knew the perfect way to do that. It meant hurting Beth, but in the long run, it was best for them both.

She took a breath. "You know I could never be with you, not with that." She pointed vaguely to Beth's heart. She watched Beth's eyes widen, as her remarks hit home.

"You're saying that because I'm scarred you could never be attracted to me?"

Kathleen only nodded, hoping Beth couldn't see the lie in her eyes. Scars or not, Kathleen was undeniably attracted to Beth. She wanted nothing more than to lay down with her and spend hours making love and holding her.

Beth stared at her for a moment, her gaze unflinching. She stood and walked toward Kathleen, forcing her to back up until her butt hit the kitchen counter. She grabbed Kathleen's hand and drew it under her T-shirt, skimming her breast, and resting it on top of the hard-ridged skin of her scar. Kathleen felt her hand tense as it touched the roughened area above Beth's heart. She wasn't repulsed by the injury. Her fingers were inches away from Beth's breast.

"This doesn't define who I am," Beth whispered fiercely. "If all you can see when you look at me is this, then you're a fool." She let go of Kathleen's hand and stepped back. Her glaring gaze bored straight into Kathleen's soul, then her features relaxed and she smiled slightly. "Tell me what you see."

Kathleen wet her lips, her heart pounding. "I can't." How could she tell Beth how perfect she was? How just the very sight of her made her palms itch to touch her, that her legs trembled with the urge to run to her? That being in her very presence settled something within her she didn't even know needed calming. Kathleen couldn't put into words everything she felt when she looked at Beth, because there weren't enough words in the world to form the portrayal. That was exactly why this was all a bad idea. A very bad idea. Beth needed someone better, someone who could love her whole heartedly. That couldn't be Kathleen. She wasn't up to the task. Beth deserved everything. Kathleen could only give her nothing.

Beth shook her head slowly and stepped closer. She cupped Kathleen's cheek with a gentle hand. "Tell me what you see when you look at me."

Kathleen stared at her for a few long moments, before one word slipped through her lips uncensored. "Hope."

Beth blinked, as if that was the last thing she expected Kathleen to say. She smiled and dropped her hand. "It's not over. I know you're scared. I won't rush you. But don't ever make me feel ashamed for what happened with Darren, ever again. This is the last time you get to use that as an excuse to run away from me. Whatever is going on, I'm here for you, when you're ready."

Kathleen had no idea she was so transparent. In the boardroom, she was a star. She could bluff her way out of any situation with her clients, but somehow, Beth had seen through her charade and straight to the heart of her duplicity. Somehow, within a few short weeks, Beth had come to know that Kathleen was running from something in her past she had never dealt with. Something that, even now, Kathleen couldn't open her mind to.

"I'm sorry." She lowered her head.

"It's okay. It's late. We should go back to bed."

Beth turned to walk away, but Kathleen reached out and grasped her hand. "I'm not ready for anything to happen between us, but please know that I do want that. More than anything."

Beth leaned up and kissed her softly on the lips. "Me too. But we both have things to deal with right now, and starting a relationship isn't ideal. I would like it if we could see each other though, not just at work."

"I'd like that too." Kathleen smiled widely.

"Good. Go to bed, and I'll see you in the morning."

Kathleen pulled her forward for another brief kiss, affirming her words of interest. "Good night, Beth." She watched her creep along the hallway, amazed at how Chloe hadn't woken up with all the kissing and talking going on. *A teenager could sleep through an earthquake.*

She made her way back into Beth's room and settled under the covers, her mind replaying the events of the last forty-five minutes. Her need to be with Beth overrode her need to keep her distance. If they had any hope of forming any kind of relationship, then Kathleen needed to find a way of dealing with her past. She needed to get back in touch with Barbara Bowden. Kathleen hadn't seen her mother in over a decade.

She couldn't keep going on like this, hurting the people she loved all because she couldn't face up to the reality of what her father did to her mother and her own role in letting it continue.

Her father had been a mean drunk and often took his frustration out on Barbara. Kathleen had always known he was beating on her, but she had never done anything to stop him. She turned a blind eye to it all and concentrated on her schoolwork, making sure she was educated enough to be able to find a decent job and get out. She found she had a good brain for numbers, maths class always being her favourite. She finished university a year early and came home to find her dad attacking her mother in one of his drunken rampages. Barbara was lying on the floor. He repeatedly kicked her in the stomach. Kathleen didn't know at the time that her mother was pregnant, and her father was trying to make her miscarry. Barbara's eyes pled with Kathleen to make him stop, but Kathleen shook her head and walked out the front door. She allowed him to put Barbara in the hospital, losing the baby as he planned, and never told a soul.

Kathleen had regretted that choice all her life. As a child, she hadn't wanted to be on the receiving end of one of his tirades. As she got older, turning a blind eye became second nature. She had failed her mother. Kathleen never went home after that and never saw her mother again, even when he passed away ten years ago. She knew Barbara still lived in the same house, but Kathleen could never find the courage to go see her. She couldn't forgive herself for walking away.

That decision shaped her into the cold person she had become. That's why she couldn't cope with Meredith's ordeal and struggled to face what had happened to Beth. If they were to have any future together, Kathleen would need to confront her mother and try and make amends for all she had done to her.

CHAPTER ELEVEN

The following morning, Beth sat in her office going over the initial plans for the winter ball. Due to Kathleen's donation, they were able to hire a hall and a band to play for the evening, although at a discounted price. The event was set to take place in eight weeks, and anticipation of the evening thrilled Beth. This was the first time she had direct control over an event like this, and she was determined to make it a success.

As she worked steadily throughout the morning, she couldn't help her lips stretching into a grin. Thoughts of her kitchen encounter with Kathleen played through her mind. Never in a million years did she think she would actually have the guts to make a move on Kathleen. She hadn't planned to, but seeing her cast in the hallway's shadow had opened a need in Beth that only Kathleen could satisfy. The kiss had been amazing, and powerful. Beth had never experienced a kiss like that before. Just recalling it sent a wave of arousal through her body and caused goose bumps to rise on her skin. It was electric and something Beth was desperate to do again.

Harsh words wound through her mind and soured her thoughts. Beth couldn't believe Kathleen would say such a horrible thing. *Isn't that what she did to Meredith? Kathleen warned you; she isn't a nice person. It's my own fault for coming on to her.* The look in Kathleen's eyes as she spoke had belied her intentions. Beth knew, without a doubt, Kathleen was lying. The words hurt nonetheless. It would have been easy to throw her out of the house and never speak to her again. Through the dimness, wounded eyes stared back at Beth and she could see the shame and guilt in Kathleen's features. Beth's intuitive thoughts lingered. She just knew there was something Kathleen was hiding, something painful. Beth wanted to help her deal with whatever it was.

Movement by her open door caught her eye. She looked up and saw her mechanic wiping his hands on an old rag. Danny was a handsome man, about thirty-five, with a smile that would have any woman, or man, twisted around his finger. For Beth though, there was nothing, not an iota of attraction.

"Hey, Danny. What's the damage?" He had come by earlier. Hopefully, the car was fixed. Beth didn't have the funds to buy a new one, so she hoped it was nothing serious.

Danny stepped into the room, giving her his best smile. "One of your spark plugs was loose. Not sure how that happened, as they're usually good and tightened. I screwed it in and, voila, one running car."

Beth lifted her eyebrows in response. She was sure it was something more serious. "Thanks for coming out. I'm glad you didn't have to tow it or anything. What do I owe you?"

"Don't worry about it." He waved her off. "It was five minutes of work."

"But you had to come all the way out here."

"It's fine. You can buy me a cup of coffee sometime." He winked at her, then passed over her keys. "Catch you around."

Beth watched him go, shaking her head at his suggestion. As good-looking and charming as he was, he just didn't do it for her. Kathleen came to mind. Her office phone rang and disrupted the pleasant images.

"Bethany Jones, how may I help you?"

"Hi, Beth, it's Margot. I just wanted to check in with you and see how things are going. Is Kathleen working out okay?"

"Hi, Margot. Everything is going great. The fundraiser is nearly all planned, and the centre is running well. Later this week, we have a lady coming from the job centre to discuss benefits and employment with some of the clients, also a group meeting for teenagers suffering from domestic violence. It should be a busy week."

"That's good. You're doing an amazing job keeping the centre up and running. I'm glad we put you in charge. And Kathleen, how is she getting on?"

Beth involuntarily smiled. *She's working out perfectly.* "I'll be honest. I was a bit sceptical at first, but she has been amazing. We had a few issues with closing the night shelter and postponing evening groups, but we managed to find compromises." Beth refrained from telling Margot that she herself was the only person working the night shelter and running groups voluntarily. She didn't think Margot would let that continue. It wasn't really safe to have only one person on staff doing all the work, but Beth wouldn't let the women down. Until the investigation was over, she would keep doing what she thought was best for the community. "She's really good at juggling the money. She's also been helping out in the centre. It'll be a shame to let her go." Beth knew Kathleen was only there temporarily, until she had sorted out her head. Beth prayed that wouldn't mean she would stop seeing her. They had started something between them, and Beth wanted, no, needed to see where it could go.

"That's great to hear. Let me know if you need anything, and I'll see you at the next meeting."

"I will. Take care."

"You too."

Beth hung up the phone and checked the clock on the wall. It was nearly one o'clock. She closed down her computer and went in search of Kathleen, hoping they could have lunch together. As she rounded the corner of her office doorway, she collided with Kathleen coming the opposite way. Again, Kathleen's strong hands reached out to steady her. She gazed up into sparkling eyes and her heart rate picked up.

"You are just determined to be close to me, aren't you?" Kathleen teased.

Beth couldn't stop her skin from flushing, knowing how true Kathleen's words were. "I was coming to see if you wanted to grab some lunch," she stammered.

Kathleen flashed a quick grin and took a step back. "I was on my way to ask you the same thing." The gazed at each other for a long moment, then both laughed.

"Come on then," Beth said, leading them down the corridor.

†

Friday afternoon Kathleen was just closing down her computer and locking up her desk when a hesitant knock sounded on her door. She looked up to see Teegan standing in her doorway, shifting from foot to foot. Kathleen had known Teegan was in the centre, as she had seen her engaging with Beth and the other teenagers in the domestic violence group. She hadn't expected Teegan to seek her out.

"Hey, Teegan. Come on in." Teegan kept her head down as she walked over and sat in the chair opposite Kathleen. Her shoulders were slumped, and her hair covered most of her face, not allowing Kathleen to see her eyes. Something was clearly wrong. Kathleen didn't want to make the mistake of asking too many questions again, so instead she asked, "Did you enjoy the group?"

"It was all right." Teegan shrugged.

"Did it help in any way?"

This was going to be a very painful conversation if Kathleen had to pull the answers out of her. Teegan obviously came to her for something, so Kathleen decided to take the risk and just ask what was on her mind.

"What's going on, Teegan?" Very slowly, Teegan lifted her head and glared at Kathleen as if she resented the question. Kathleen blew out a breath. "Look, I can't help you unless you talk to me."

Teegan briefly closed her eyes then stood up. She removed her denim jacket and dumped it on the chair.

Teegan gripped the hem of her T-shirt. As she lifted her shirt, Kathleen's breath caught in her throat.

Black and blue bruises covered her ribs and led around to her back. To Kathleen, it looked like she had been stomped on. "What the hell happened?" she asked more sharply than she had intended. Teegan lowered her shirt and slumped back into the chair.

"Shane."

Kathleen looked away, unsure of how to respond. Ideally, she wanted to go get Beth. Teegan had spent all afternoon with Beth and apparently hadn't told her. *She came to me. I've got to pull it together.* She looked back at Teegan. "I'm not going to tell you to go to the police. That's your decision to make. However, I won't allow you to go back there to him."

Teegan's eyes narrowed and she scowled. "I have nowhere else to go. I can't just stay here all the time, and I refuse to go to a foster home."

It was clear that Teegan had at least a little bit of trust in Kathleen. She didn't want to do anything to harm the bond they were forming. Different options ran through Kathleen's mind before landing on the one she hoped wouldn't be a mistake. She didn't really have a choice; she couldn't let Teegan go back to Shane.

"Do you still want to be with him?"

"He's getting worse." Teegan shook her head vigorously. "Lashing out more. I don't want to be around him anymore. I'm scared he's going to kill me one day." For the first time, tears rolled down her cheeks. "I don't know what to do. Listening to Beth talk about domestic violence made me realise that I'm stuck in a trap. He promises to change but never does. I don't want this to be my life."

"I can help you, but I need to be able to trust you."

Teegan swiped at the tears on her cheeks and nodded. "I'll do anything."

"You can stay with me."

"What?"

"I have a pretty big house. There's enough room for you, but you have to promise to stay away from him.

"I will, I swear."

Kathleen studied her face, noting the sincerity there. She prayed this wasn't a stupid idea. "I'll need to talk with Beth, make sure this is okay. Are you all right with her knowing?"

Teegan nodded.

"Okay. Sit tight and I'll go find her."

As she passed Teegan, she gave her slim shoulder a gentle squeeze. She found Beth in her own office, typing on her keyboard. Even though she had only seen her a few hours ago, she still got a jolt of excitement when Beth caught her gaze. They had had lunch together every day for the last few days, and she was enjoying getting to know more about her. They had kept things casual, never venturing too deeply into the problems each had. Easing into a friendship with Beth felt nice. Kathleen still hadn't found the courage to visit her mother. If she didn't do it soon, she wouldn't be able to move into any kind of relationship with Beth. The past needed to be laid to rest. She needed to be free of her guilt.

"Hey, Beth, can I talk to you for a second?"

Beth smiled warmly at her. "Of course, come in."

"Teegan is in my office. Shane did a number on her, and her torso is heavily bruised."

"Son of a bitch! I had no idea. She was fine in group, just a bit quiet."

"I doubt she'll go to the police, but I don't want her to go back with him." She looked up at the ceiling, reaching for composure. Her anger over the abuse was swamping her objectivity. "I said she could stay with me."

"Um, are you sure that's a good idea?" Beth's eyebrows rose, clearly surprised.

"Probably not, but I just can't see her leave tonight and not know if she's going to be safe."

"I understand that, however, she can't be your responsibility. There are hundreds of people going through similar situations, and you can't help them all by yourself. That's why we arm them with all the information we can and help them move on if that's what they want."

Kathleen thought over Beth's words. She was right. If Kathleen opened her house to everyone who needed help, she would soon be over run. "I know what you're saying, and I agree. There's just something about her. I really want to help." She couldn't explain why, she just did. There was a connection to Teegan. She needed to protect her.

"She's over sixteen, so legally she can choose where to live. Officially, I don't agree with this, but personally, I think it's great you want to help her. Just be careful, okay? We don't know her full background."

"I will." Kathleen smiled her thanks, then stood to leave. As an afterthought she asked, "What are you doing this weekend?"

"I promised Chloe we'd spend some time together. She's getting pretty annoyed at being at the sitter's all the time while I work."

"Oh, okay. Well, if at some point you're free, maybe we could meet for coffee or something."

Beth smiled. "I have a better idea. Why don't you come around for pizza and a movie again? You can bring Teegan if she's up for it."

"You wouldn't mind?"

"Of course not. I like her."

"I'll see how she settles in and check with her, but count me in." She gazed at Beth for a moment, then went back to her own office. Teegan was still slumped in the chair but glanced up as Kathleen walked in.

"I checked with Beth, and she said it's okay if you want to stay with me."

"Are you sure?"

Kathleen wasn't certain about many things in her life, but this she was. "Absolutely. Is there anything you need from your place?"

"Nah, it's just clothes and stuff. I have my phone, that's all I need."

Kathleen nodded. "Okay then, let's go."

†

"You live here?" Teegan asked with wonder in her voice.

Kathleen pulled on the handbrake and looked at her house from an outsider's perspective. She lived at the end of a country lane, with no other houses around for miles. It used to be an old farmhouse, but Kathleen had spent a small fortune renovating. The result was impressive. The outside walls were painted a light blue, and neatly cut hedges lined the front garden. There were only four bedrooms, but each room was oversized. A family of six could live there and still have plenty of space so they weren't all on top of each other. For Kathleen, it showed how far she had come in her life.

She'd spent years trying to get out of the negative shadow her father had put her in. This house proved she wasn't the loser he always said she was.

"Yeah, I do. Come on, I'll show you around."

They exited the car and approached the front door. Kathleen felt her heart pounding. For some reason, she was nervous about how Teegan would perceive her living choices. She didn't want Teegan to think all she cared about was money. Although, that was pretty much all Kathleen had cared about in the past, until the whole thing with Meredith happened.

She unlocked the door and ushered Teegan inside. Teegan stood still in the large foyer, only her wide eyes climbed the twisting staircase up to the first floor. A large lounge covered the left-hand side of the property and led out to the back garden. A baby grand piano sat by the patio doors, and a huge, stone fireplace commanded centre stage. Kathleen waited in the foyer, as Teegan wandered around slowly, apparently taking it all in. She crossed to the right-hand side of the building toward the kitchen, where she would find high-end cabinets bound by granite countertops. A double fridge and work island were also of the highest quality. Kathleen lowered her head, all of a sudden feeling ashamed for the money she had spent. She didn't know why. Perhaps it was knowing Teegan had literally nothing to her name.

"Holy shit, you're loaded," Teegan said, as she walked back into the foyer.

Heat suffused Kathleen's cheeks and she shrugged. Teegan didn't need to know she was nearly a millionaire.

Teegan must have sensed her discomfort. "Are you sure you want me staying here?"

"I wouldn't have asked if I wasn't sure." She grasped Teegan's arm and led her up the stairs to the first floor. She pointed out the bathroom, her office, and bedroom as they walked down the hallway. "Your room will be here." She opened the spare room door wide and allowed Teegan to pass in front of her. This room held a four-poster bed and dresser. The window overlooked the fields behind the house. Teegan went to the window and stood looking out at the view for a few moments.

"My only rules are that Shane doesn't ever come here and you clean up after yourself."

Teegan turned, tears clinging to her eyelashes. "Why would you want to help me? Why would you allow the likes of me in your beautiful home?"

The question should have shocked Kathleen, but it didn't. She'd been asking herself the same question since they left the centre. She took Teegan's hand and led her to the bed, sitting down side by side. She took a moment to think of her reply, knowing that only the truth would suffice.

"When I was a kid growing up, we had nothing. My mum didn't work, and my dad was an asshole. I felt adrift from them and spent most of my time out with friends, studying, drinking, and partying. I didn't even care when my dad would hit my mum. When I reached twenty-one, I'd finally had enough, and I left." She didn't mention the final event that triggered her leaving. Teegan didn't need to know those gory details. "I worked my ass off in university and found I had a talent for numbers. I've known hard times and spent twenty years working my way up to be where I am today. It wasn't always easy. Many nights, I went without food and electric just to pay my rent." She took a breath then wiped away the tear that rolled down Teegan's cheek. "I always wished I had someone fighting in my corner, to help me succeed, so it wouldn't have been so hard. You've had a horrible time of it so far, and I just want to give you the chance I never got. You deserve to have someone fighting in your corner."

"Thanks for saying that, but how do you know I'm not going to rip you off, steal all your stuff?"

"I don't trust easily. If you want to take anything, then go for it. I can afford to replace every single item in this house. I'm just hoping my trust and faith in you will be enough that you respect my home. And respect yourself."

Teegan sat quietly for a minute, her gaze travelling around the room as if seeing through the walls to the rest of the house. Eventually, she held Kathleen's hand and said, "I won't let you down, thank you."

Kathleen smiled and squeezed Teegan's fingers. "Okay. I don't know about you, but I'm starving. Let's go find something to eat."

They headed down to the kitchen and pulled together ingredients to make a lasagne and garlic bread. Kathleen thought over her words to Teegan. It was true she, could replace everything. There was nothing sentimental to her in the home, except for a photo of her and Meredith at a charity event taken some years before. Everything else was just stuff. She hoped by being honest with Teegan and laying her trust in her, that Teegan wouldn't be tempted. Beth was right, they didn't know her history. Kathleen prayed that the fact Teegan came to her about her bruises signified a trust that wouldn't be swayed by shiny objects. Kathleen had good instincts about people, and she knew, deep down, Teegan could be trusted.

CHAPTER TWELVE

Sunday evening found Kathleen relaxing comfortably on Beth's sofa, beer in hand, as she watched Teegan and Chloe racing each other on Mario Kart. Beth was in the kitchen clearing up after their dinner. She had refused Kathleen's help, forcing her to stay in the lounge and out from underfoot. It had been a great few hours. Teegan was originally unsure about coming with her, but Kathleen had promised that Beth was looking forward to seeing her. A good move on Beth's part, Teegan and Chloe hit it off right away despite their five-year age difference. A pleasant feeling suffused Kathleen, a soft smile overtaking her lips. *This must be what it's like to have a family.* The thought flittered through her mind and her eyes went wide. She had never imagined family was something she ever wanted or was capable of having, but she enjoyed the hope it brought to her heart. Maybe she was capable of love. Her mother's face came to mind and slammed the door on her joy. If Kathleen didn't go and see her soon, she wouldn't be able to fully forgive herself.

Past memories were not allowed to spoil her good mood. She stood and stretched, then went in search of Beth. She found her sitting at the kitchen table, staring at her mobile phone. Her lips were pursed, and frown lines marred her usually smooth forehead. She didn't seem to notice Kathleen standing in the doorway.

"You okay?"

Beth blinked and looked up, then smiled softly. "Yeah. I got another hang-up call on my phone. That's the fifth one this week."

Kathleen glanced over her shoulder to make sure they were still alone. She sat next to Beth, taking her hand in her own. She had a good idea of what was going on, and it didn't sit well in her gut. "What are you thinking?"

Beth turned wounded eyes to Kathleen. "I think it's Darren." Tears filled her eyes and tumbled down her cheeks. "What do I do if he's found me?"

Kathleen gathered her in her arms and tucked her head under her chin, into her favourite hug. She tried to settle her own racing heart, knowing Beth needed her to be strong. This wasn't the time to show her the rage she felt inside. "First thing tomorrow, you need to call your solicitor. Get him to contact Darren's probation officer. They might be able to find out if it's him, or at least give him a warning. Have you thought about changing your number?"

Beth pulled away. She shook her head as she wiped her eyes. "I can't. The women have my number, and I'm now the first point of contact for emergencies. I'll never be able to contact everyone who might have my business card. It'll be too much work."

Kathleen took a breath. She knew Beth was right but hated the circumstances. If Darren did have Beth's number, how long would it be until he found her address?

"What was that?" Beth's gaze focused on Kathleen.

"Huh?

"Your body just shook, and your eyes turned nearly black."

That would be rage. Of course, she didn't tell Beth that. She didn't need her to know how much hate was flowing through her body. Kathleen had no doubt that if she ever saw Darren anywhere near Beth, she would kill him. She pulled Beth close once again and kissed her temple. "It was nothing, don't worry." Beth didn't question her further, but Kathleen knew she didn't believe her answer.

It was time to salvage the rest of the evening. "Do you fancy getting your ass kicked at Mario Kart?"

Beth chuckled. "I'll play, but you won't win."

"We'll see."

The evening wore on, and eventually it was time for Kathleen and Teegan to go. They said their goodbyes to Chloe, and Beth walked them out to Kathleen's car. It didn't escape Kathleen's notice that Beth's gaze quickly darted around the property as they exited the house. Teegan got into the passenger side and closed her door, leaving Kathleen and Beth in relative privacy.

"We had a good time tonight," Kathleen said. "Thank you for inviting us."

Beth smiled and took her hand. "Thank you for coming. Sorry about earlier."

Kathleen shook her head and gave her a quick hug. "Never apologise for that. We'll figure out what's going on."

Beth nodded and stepped back. "I'll see you tomorrow at work."

"Yes." Kathleen hesitated a moment, then leaned forward. She kissed Beth gently on the cheek. For the casual observer, it would look like a quick kiss between friends, but for Kathleen, it was much more. It was a promise of things to come. Beth's skin flushed, and Kathleen knew she felt the meaning behind the simple gesture. She opened her door and slid inside. "I'll wait until you're back in the house." Beth nodded her thanks, before she turned and strode up the path. She didn't look back until she had the front door open and she was on the other side of the threshold. She waved goodbye and shut the door. Kathleen started the car and pulled away.

The drive back to her house was made in relative silence until Teegan asked, "What's going on with you and Beth?"

The question caught Kathleen off guard. They had been careful not to be too obvious. They'd sat on opposite ends of the sofa and kept a distance from each other. Kathleen thought they'd pulled off the friend routine, but evidently Teegan had picked up on something. Kathleen cleared her throat. "What do you mean?"

"Come on. Anyone with eyes can see you have the hots for each other."

Damn. Kathleen wasn't closeted, but she knew this was the first time Beth had acted on her feelings since acknowledging her sexuality. Kathleen didn't want to betray Beth's trust, so she refrained from admitting anything and hoped Teegan would let it drop. "We're friends," she said, shrugging slightly.

"I'm not going to cause any trouble for you, you know."

Kathleen could hear the pout in her voice. She knew she could trust Teegan, but it wasn't just her feelings she had to consider. "Teegan, yes, I'm a lesbian, and I have a little crush on Beth, but that's all." She hated diminishing her feelings for Beth as just a crush, but it was the only way to protect Beth while allowing Teegan into her life a little.

"It's more than that, and Beth feels the same. It's obvious. Don't worry, I won't tell anyone."

Teegan was more perceptive than Kathleen gave her credit for. She was a smart young woman. Kathleen just knew, with the right amount of support, Teegan could achieve anything. She blew out a breath.

"Look, there is a lot going on right now, and we're just kinda feeling each other out." Teegan snorted and Kathleen blushed. "Not like that. You know what I mean. We're taking it slow. Neither one of us wants to be hurt."

Teegan was quiet for a moment. "Chloe told me about her dad, about what he did to Beth."

"She did?" From what Beth had said, Chloe hadn't talked about the event that nearly killed her mother. She was glad Chloe felt she could trust Teegan and had someone she could confide in. It was a start to her healing that Kathleen had no doubt she needed.

"Yeah. I had no idea Beth had been through that. Chloe is worried he might be coming back."

"We don't know anything yet, but Beth is worried too."

Teegan reached out and grasped Kathleen's forearm where it rested on the centre console. "We're not going to let him hurt them, are we?"

Teegan had said the words with such venom and ferocity that it stunned Kathleen for a moment. "No. No, we're not."

116

"Good. And for the record, I think you and Beth make a cute couple."

"It doesn't bother you we're both women?"

"Kath, I'm a teenager," she said, as if that explained it all.

"Good to know."

After a few minutes of silence, driving through the darkened streets, Teegan asked, "Is it okay if I come to the centre with you tomorrow?"

"Sure, if you want. I might have to work late, so you could be there a long time."

"That's fine, I like being there."

Me too. That admission to herself should have scared Kathleen, but it didn't. She found work at the centre rewarding, and the lethargy she had felt in the months leading up to her sabbatical was now absent. She would need to start thinking about her future and what she seriously wanted out of it.

CHAPTER THIRTEEN

It was Monday afternoon, and Beth sat with her elbows on her desk, head in her hands. She had called Graham first thing in the morning, asking if he could confirm Darren was still up north. After calling Darren's probation officer, Graham had called back. He didn't have good news, and Beth felt like her world was imploding. Her thoughts were a jumbled mess. *I'll have to move again. But I don't want to leave here.* Two months ago, she wouldn't have thought twice about packing up and leaving. Now she had met Kathleen, and Kathleen meant something to her. Her attraction was getting stronger every day, and she didn't want to give that up. She might not have a choice. Chloe would always come first. She hoped Kathleen would understand.

A hesitant knock on her door startled Beth from her ruminations. "Come in." She pasted on her most brilliant smile, so whoever needed to see her wouldn't know she was on the verge of a breakdown. The door opened and Kathleen walked in. She studied Beth. One look into Kathleen's calm, blue gaze was her undoing, and tears burst from Beth's eyes. She found herself being guided up from her chair and engulfed in a tight hug. Kathleen murmured words of comfort into her ear.

"I'm sorry," Beth mumbled into Kathleen's chest. She felt Kathleen hold her tighter.

"It's okay. What happened?"

Beth pulled back but remained in the circle of Kathleen's arms. She looked up, seeing understanding and compassion. She could look into those eyes for the rest of her life. The realisation she might never see them again nearly had her doubling over in grief. She took a breath to steady herself.

"My solicitor called me back a little while ago. Darren's probation officer hasn't seen him for over two weeks. The police went to his house and found his ankle tag on the kitchen table. There's a warrant out for him. He's gone."

Kathleen hugged her again and let her cry. "Mother fucker."

"He's here, isn't he?"

"I don't know, Beth. What are you going to do?"

Beth stepped back fully, needing the distance from Kathleen's strong presence. She didn't want to say these words, but she had no choice. "Same as I did last time. Disappear." A flash of pain shot across Kathleen's face. She doubled over, clutching her stomach. Feeling behind her, she found Beth's chair and slumped into it. She gazed up at Beth, anguish clear in her eyes.

119

"You can't."

Beth knelt in front of her and grasped her tight fists where they rested on the arms of the chair. "I have no choice. I can't let him find me. I have to keep Chloe safe." She thought for a second then said, "You could come with us. I know we've only just started to get to know each other, but I don't want to lose you. I feel connected to you. I need you."

Kathleen reached out and gently cupped her cheek, regret marring her features. "I need you too, more than you know, but running away isn't the answer. We can fight him. Get him arrested if he shows up."

Beth shook her head. "All it takes is a few seconds to kill me or take Chloe. I can't risk it."

"We still don't know he's here. We could be worrying over nothing."

Beth stood and paced, as much as she could in the small office. She thought back over the phone calls, the eerie feeling she felt every time she got home, her car not starting. She might be paranoid, but she knew in her gut he was there, watching her. She stopped pacing and faced Kathleen.

"No, he's here. It's only a matter of time before he strikes. I need to start making plans." Her heart broke, as a lone tear rolled down Kathleen's cheek. She went to her and pulled her up, wiping the tear away with her thumb. "I'm sorry," she said, before she leaned in and kissed Kathleen with all she had in her. Kathleen melted against her, her hands slipping into her hair and holding her close. The kiss was hard, filled with a passion Beth didn't know she possessed. She didn't want it to be a kiss goodbye, but she feared that was exactly what it was. They pulled back from each other, both crying freely now.

"When will you go?" Kathleen asked, her voice cracking.

"It'll probably take me a couple of weeks to sort some things out." She would need to get in contact with Brian. He had sorted out her new identification last time. She needed to find a place to live, somewhere remote. "Chloe will need to be taken out of school and have to come here with me every day."

"She can hang around with Teegan. She'll keep an eye on her."

Kathleen's eyes took on a predatory look. Beth knew this must be how Kathleen looked in the boardroom. The determination and focus in her features turned Beth on. Kathleen was a strong woman, but also tender and caring. Beth breathed deeply to calm her racing heart.

"I'm going to call a friend. He works security. I'll get him to send someone down here to keep an eye on the premises, make sure Darren doesn't show up."

"The centre can't afford that." Beth loved Kathleen's protective side, but knew the state of the accounts wouldn't allow such a thing.

"The centre won't be paying. I will."

Beth blinked, not sure she'd heard right. "I can't let you do that."

"You don't get a choice. I'm not going to let him get to you. Money isn't an issue, and this is non-negotiable."

"Thank you." Beth should have been annoyed at Kathleen's presumptions. However, she was thrilled Kathleen was willing to do whatever it took to keep her safe.

"I'll make sure it's a woman, so the clients won't be afraid."

"You really are remarkable." Even in the midst of this crisis, Kathleen was still thinking about the centre. Beth wondered if she knew how good a fit she was to this place. "Will you be okay if I head off to collect Chloe?"

"Of course. I'll have Teegan help Fran clear up the kitchen and get started on the cleaning." She grinned. "She said she liked being here, but I imagine she enjoyed just hanging out. An afternoon of cleaning might change her mind."

"You're evil."

"Yep." They laughed, and Beth was pleased the joke had loosened some of the tension that had sprung up in her body since Graham called. "Has she heard from Shane at all?"

"No. Last time she saw him, he was really high and drunk. She said he probably hasn't realised she's gone yet."

"I'm pleased you'll get someone here to watch the place. It'll help if Shane, or anyone else, shows up. Maybe once the investigation into the accounts is over, the board might see to making security full time." Beth gathered her coat and bag and glanced around the office to make sure she hadn't forgotten anything. Gazing back at Kathleen, she said, "Right, I need to go."

"Be safe."

"I will." Beth took a step forward and kissed her again, slowly this time. "I'm sorry about all this." Life was cruel. Just when she had finally begun to move on with her life, to finally think happiness could be in her future, it was being ripped away from her yet again. She hated to see the heartbreak in Kathleen's face, but it needed to be done. Chloe came first. "I'll see you tomorrow."

†

Kathleen sat back down in Beth's vacated chair, her body vibrating with tension. She couldn't believe that evil prick had gone AWOL and was quite possibly coming after Beth. The thought of losing her now, after she had finally begun to feel normal again, terrified Kathleen. There was nothing she could do, though, to stop her leaving. She didn't blame Beth for wanting to escape to somewhere safer. She thought over the offer to go with her. It was a crazy notion. Once Beth knew the real Kathleen, she wouldn't want her around. Uprooting her life and following Beth just to be sent away wouldn't make sense. She had a life here. *It isn't the best right now.* She didn't have many friends and her job was in jeopardy, but the last few weeks working for the centre had allowed her to assess herself. She had time to dig herself out of the hole she'd been in. No, following Beth wasn't an option. Getting Beth to stay would be the better plan. She knew Beth liked living here. She valued her job and was settled. Kathleen also knew that Chloe liked the school she was in and had lots of friends. No way would she want to leave. Kathleen needed to find a way to persuade Beth to stay and to get Darren out of her life for good. She just didn't know how.

Teegan strode into the office, her forehead creasing when she saw Kathleen. "I was looking for Beth."

"She had to leave. Close the door and sit down a minute. I need to talk to you."

Teegan did as asked, her gaze wary as she sat down. "You're not kicking me out already are you?"

"What? God no. It has to do with Beth."

"Did you screw up already?" Teegan lifted her eyebrows, her lips set in a tight line.

Teegan's comment made Kathleen smile. "No, but things will probably have to take a back seat for a while." It really did suck that they couldn't continue to grow closer in the way they would both have liked. Kathleen knew Beth wouldn't want to get involved, despite the kiss they'd shared earlier, now her mind was set on leaving. She couldn't blame Beth for that, but Kathleen was determined to stop her from going. She just needed a plan to flush Darren out before he could hurt anyone. "Beth thinks her ex-husband is…I guess you could say stalking her."

"Fuck." At Kathleen's raised eyebrows she said, "Sorry. I meant, oh no."

"The probation office which is in charge of his release haven't seen him for a couple of weeks, and Beth is convinced he's here." She wondered if she should be telling Teegan all this. It was clear Teegan respected Beth and liked her. She also clearly liked Chloe. Kathleen could see the determination in Teegan's gaze and knew she would help any way she could. "Over the last few weeks, Beth has received a few nuisance calls and sometimes feels she's being watched. I'm not sure if it's her paranoia acting up of if there really is a threat. She's pulling Chloe from school, so she'll be here from now on until they leave."

"Leave? What do you mean?"

"Beth's real name isn't Beth. After the incident, she changed her name and fled from up north. She wants to do the same again."

Teegan shot up from her chair, her cheeks flushed with anger. "That's crazy. This place will fall apart without her. She can't just leave."

"Teegan, sit down."

Teegan complied and ran her hand through her hair. "I happen to agree with you. We need to do what we can to make her feel safe. Hopefully, once Darren is caught and sent back to prison, she'll see reason."

"But even if he did go back, he'll get out again. She'll always be afraid of him."

Teegan had just put to voice the one thing Kathleen dreaded. Beth would always be running. It wasn't a nice feeling, always being scared of your past, fearing you could never escape. Kathleen knew that feeling well and didn't want the same for Beth.

"I'm not sure how we can change that, but for now, we need to keep them safe."

"I'll help any way I can."

"I know, thank you. As I said, Chloe will be here every day. I want you to stick by her, keep an eye out for her. I'm going to get a security guard on site, but she won't be able to be everywhere at once. I'll need you to protect Chloe. If Darren is hanging around, I don't want him to have access to her."

"I won't let you, or Beth, down."

Kathleen nodded. She knew she could trust Teegan to do whatever it took to keep Chloe safe. While she was doing that, Kathleen would be keeping an eye on Beth. With an immediate plan of action in place, Kathleen gave Teegan a list of jobs to fill the afternoon with and went back to her office. All the while, thoughts of Beth leaving and her safety plagued her mind.

CHAPTER FOURTEEN

History was on replay. Beth followed Chloe into the house, watching her throw her bag onto the sofa and flop down next to it. Chloe was none too happy to be pulled from school again, and Beth knew it was only going to get worse when she found out she wouldn't be going back. It was time they talked about what happened five years ago, and what was going to happen now.

Beth went into the kitchen and brought back a chair, placing it in front of Chloe so they could see each other eye to eye. She reached over and took Chloe's phone from her hands, ignoring her scowl. "We need to talk," she said, having no clue how to start. Chloe glowered Beth idly wondered if Chloe was ever going to stop being sullen with her. Ever since the stabbing, Chloe had been distant. Beth didn't think it was just because of the trauma. She couldn't help thinking Chloe blamed her in some way. She took a breath. "You remember I told you your father was out of prison?" Chloe looked away and nodded. "Well, now he's gone missing. I think he might be in Bristol and watching us." She didn't quite know how to say the next thing, so she blurted it out. "We have to move." Beth flinched when Chloe shot off the couch.

"No! I don't want to. I like it here."

"I do too, honey, but it's for our own safety that we leave." She grasped Chloe's hand, noting it was cold. "He's dangerous. I can't let him near us again."

Chloe collapsed back onto the sofa, flipping her hair out of her eyes. "How can he be here? We changed our names and stuff."

"I don't know. There are ways of finding out information. It could be something as simple as my address on the restraining order. For it to be legal, he would need to know what areas to stay out of."

"Do you really think he'd try hurting you again?" Chloe's gaze fixed onto the carpet, avoiding Beth. "I don't want that to happen."

"Chloe, you've never spoken about what happened. Is there any reason for that? I don't want the past affecting you in ways you can't handle when you're older." Beth tried to ignore thoughts of Chloe turning to drugs to combat her feelings. She wouldn't be able to forgive herself if something like that happened, all because her father couldn't handle getting a divorce.

Chloe shrugged, still not looking up. "I still have dreams about it. All the blood. I don't think it'll ever go away." Tears rolled slowly down her cheeks as she spoke. "I don't understand how he could do that to you, and to me. He must have known I would be coming home that morning and would find you. How could he let me walk into that?"

Beth gathered Chloe into her arms, holding her close. How could she explain his monstrous act? She couldn't even blame it on a mental disorder. The courts had found him sane. He had shown no remorse and even smiled at Beth when he was sentenced. He was evil, pure and simple. She couldn't tell Chloe that. He was still her father, and Beth didn't want Chloe to grow up thinking she could be like him because they shared DNA.

"I don't think he was thinking. He was angry and lashed out."

"And you think he still is? Angry, I mean."

Beth's mind once again thought over the phone calls and the suddenly loose spark plug. A thought struck her so hard she felt it in her gut. Was Darren watching that day? If Kathleen hadn't left work when she did, would he have attacked? *Would I be dead right now?* It was a disquieting feeling.

"I think there is a good possibility he still wants me gone."

Chloe cried harder and clung to Beth. Between sobs, she said, "Okay, we can go."

"Thank you, baby." She smoothed Chloe's hair. "You can't go back to school. You'll have to come to work with me until I can figure out what we're going to do."

"Should you even go there, if he's around?"

Beth pondered the question. If she was leaving anyway, then she really didn't need to go back. She wanted to help the women as much as she could before she left. And of course, seeing Kathleen every day would be an added bonus. She wanted to spend as much time with her as possible, as selfish as that was. Her chance at happiness was slipping away, and she hated the idea that she would probably never Kathleen again.

"Kath is getting a security guard to watch the place, so we'll be safe. Also, Teegan will be there, so you two can hang out with each other." That brought a tentative smile to Chloe's lips.

"She's cool."

"Yeah, she is."

Beth glanced at the clock mounted by the TV. "Why don't you change out of your uniform, while I'll make a couple of calls. Then we can watch a movie or something before dinner."

"Okay." Chloe stepped out of Beth's arms, running her hand over her face to rid it of her tears. "I'm sorry, Mum."

A look of guilt flashed over Chloe's features before quickly being hidden. It struck Beth as odd, but she couldn't fathom why Chloe would be apologising. She chalked it up to Chloe perhaps feeling some misplaced responsibility in the attack. "It's okay. We'll be fine."

Chloe picked up her bag, then headed off to her room. Beth stood from her chair and carried it back to the kitchen. Pulling her phone from her pocket, she searched for the contact she never thought she would have to use again. She hoped the number was still in use. It was answered on the fourth ring.

"Brian, it's Hannah Kirkdale. I need your help again."

†

Six o'clock rolled around, and someone knocked at Beth's front door. A sense of dread filled her stomach, as she tentatively stepped toward the door. It was an irrational fear. Darren wouldn't knock. She pressed against the wood and looked through the peephole, smiling when she saw Kathleen and a very anxious looking Teegan standing on the other side. She unlocked the door and pulled it wide.

"Hey, guys," Beth said.

"Are you okay?" Teegan's gaze darted around the room behind Beth as if looking for danger.

Beth took her hand to try and settle her. "We're fine. Come on in. Chloe's in her room if you want to go see her." Teegan didn't need to be asked twice and set off in a rush to find her. It was sweet how much Teegan cared for her daughter. She turned back to Kathleen. "Chloe always wanted a big sister."

"Teegan couldn't wait for me to close up the centre so we could come check on you guys."

"My little knight in shining armour. You fit that description also." Beth gaped as Kathleen's demeanour shifted and she broke down in tears. "Oh God, what's wrong?" Beth pulled Kathleen to her.

"You can't go. You can't leave me."

Kathleen clung to her, and it shook Beth how upset she was. Kathleen had always appeared strong. She didn't think her leaving would affect her so much. But of course it would; it affected Beth the same way.

"I don't have a choice. Let's just enjoy how long we have left."

Kathleen disentangled herself from Beth. Her eyes narrowed. Anger was vibrating off her. "How can you let him get away with this? You'll always be running."

Beth hugged herself against Kathleen's harsh words. It wasn't like she was doing this willingly. Did Kathleen think she enjoyed always looking over her shoulder? Of course she didn't, but it was the only way to keep her family safe.

"If you can't accept this, then perhaps you should just go now. I won't change my mind." Kathleen was breathing hard, and Beth could see her visibly trying to calm down. She wanted to leave on good terms. Fighting with her wasn't the way to do that, but she wouldn't be swayed. Her control had been taken away once, she wouldn't let that happen again.

Kathleen took a shuddering breath. "I don't want to lose you," she whispered.

"Me either, but it is what it is." She reached out and grasped her hand, entwining their fingers. "I was just about to make popcorn and watch a film. You and Teegan are welcome to stay and watch with us."

"Try and stop me."

As they set about making snacks and choosing what movie to watch, talk of Beth's departure remained closed. Beth wanted a normal evening, when all the bad stuff in her life wasn't present. She wanted to enjoy the night, because she wasn't sure it would ever happen again. Brian had started his work on fixing her two new identities. She knew from experience it wouldn't be long before he was ready. This night would probably be the only time she could relax with Kathleen and not have it be marred with heartbreak and loss. She was determined to make it so.

After the film was chosen and the snacks dispensed between them, Beth sat next to Kathleen on the sofa. Teegan and Chloe sat in front of them on the carpet. Beth pressed play and the DVD started. She felt something touch her hand

and glanced down to see Kathleen wrapping her hand around her own, giving it a tight squeeze. She turned her head to look at her.

"Sorry," Kathleen mouthed, her forehead creasing.

Beth mouthed back, "It's okay," knowing she was apologising for her earlier outburst. It touched Beth deeply that Kathleen cared so much about her to try and stop her leaving. She glanced at Chloe and Teegan, engrossed in the film. Beth leaned toward Kathleen and kissed her gently on the lips. Kathleen smiled, and they turned their attention back to the film.

About halfway through, Beth's phone buzzed with an incoming call from where it sat on the arm of the sofa. Joyce, Chloe's sitter, flashed on the screen. Beth paused the film and answered, thinking she wanted to arrange when Chloe would be staying again. Her thoughts couldn't be farther from the truth. She felt the colour drain from her face as she listened, her body trembling. Kathleen must have sensed something was wrong, as she scooted closer and wrapped her arm around Beth's waist, holding her near. She hung up after the call, her mind whirling with a million thoughts. They all led back to Darren.

"What's happened?"

Beth took a moment to gather herself. "That was Joyce, Chloe's sitter. Her house was vandalised. Broken windows and smashed flowerpots. The words *I'm coming* were spray painted onto a wall." She was amazed her voice came out as calmly as it did. It had to be Darren. "Darren must know that's where Chloe goes. He's watching us." She looked at Chloe. Teegan had gathered her close, fear evident in her face. What would have happened if Chloe had gone there after school instead of Beth picking her up early? Would

Darren have abducted her? She recoiled at the thought. "It has to be him." She looked back at Kathleen. "We need to leave. Now." She stood from the sofa and ran her hands through her hair, trying to figure out what she was going to do. *Pack a bag, essentials, get to a hotel out of town, get as far from here as possible.*

"Beth, calm down," Kathleen said. "We don't know it's him."

She whirled around. "Don't be an idiot, of course it's him." Her gaze went to the lounge window. "He could be watching us right now." She went to the blinds and carefully peeked through a gap, scanning the front garden and the street beyond. Kathleen stood behind her with a hand on her shoulder.

"Teegan, take Chloe into her room and help her pack some things."

"Okay."

"Beth. Look at me, Beth."

Beth lowered the slat of the blind and turned. "What?"

"You're scaring Chloe," she said kindly. "You need to calm down."

"How can I be calm? He could be here."

Kathleen cupped her cheek, gazing intently at her. "I know. I'm not going to let anything happen to you. Go pack some things. You and Chloe are coming home with me. We'll call the police once we get there."

Beth shook her head. She wouldn't allow Darren anywhere near Kathleen. "No. You can't be involved in this. I won't let him hurt you."

"God damn it, Beth. I am involved. I love you. Let me protect you."

Beth froze. Every thought left her head. "What?" Surely she had misheard.

"That wasn't supposed to come out." Kathleen glanced away. "It doesn't make it any less true. I can't explain it, and I don't want to, but I can't walk away from this, from you. Not now. Please let me help."

To say Beth was dumbfounded would be an understatement. Yeah, they were attracted to each other, but love? They had only known each other for a month. Wasn't that too soon to be feeling that kind of emotion? She gazed at Kathleen, knowing in her heart she felt the same. However, this wasn't the time to be getting into all that. Her crazy ex was coming for her.

"Are you sure about this? It's going to be dangerous."

"I don't care."

Beth warred within herself. Would it really be fair to let Kathleen and Teegan take this risk for her? No, it wasn't fair, but she found herself agreeing. She didn't want to bare this burden alone any longer. "Okay. But we need to make sure he doesn't follow us, if he is watching."

They set about packing up what essentials they needed, and Kathleen carried them to her car. When she came back inside, she asked Teegan, "Do you know how to drive?"

"Not legally, but yeah."

Kathleen nodded. "Good enough." She tossed Teegan her keys. "You take my car and drive Beth and Chloe home. Take lots of different turns. Double back and check you're not being followed."

Teegan nodded.

"What about you?" Beth asked.

"I'm going to hang back a minute and follow in your car, to make sure he isn't behind. Between us, we should get home without any trouble. If you see anything suspicious, ring the police right away."

Beth stepped up to Kathleen and lowered her voice. "I don't like this."

"It'll be fine. Just go with Teegan and be careful."

Knowing that Kathleen wouldn't change her mind, Beth nodded and hugged her briefly. She held out her hand. "Come on, Chloe." After quickly scanning the street, she made a beeline for Kathleen's car, pulling Chloe along with her.

CHAPTER FIFTEEN

Kathleen entered the kitchen, her feet dragging on the tile. The adrenalin of the last hour and a half was now dissipating, and she felt heavy and tired. A drive that should have taken thirty minutes to her house from Beth's took them nearly an hour. The stress of making sure no one followed Teegan had taken its toll. Kathleen still wasn't a hundred percent certain it was Darren doing all this, but it was getting harder to dispute. The important thing was that Beth believed it. Kathleen would do what it took to help Beth feel safe. Teegan was at the kitchen island making sandwiches. "Hey." Teegan looked up and smiled.

"Hi."

Kathleen swiped a slice of cheese to munch on. "You did a good job getting them here." She reached up and squeezed

Teegan's shoulder. "Thank you." Teegan blushed. Kathleen lifted an eyebrow. "I won't ask how it is you know how to drive without a licence."

"When your life doesn't have rules, you learn things pretty quick." Teegan shrugged and put the lid back on the mayo.

Kathleen watched Teegan finish plating up two sandwiches she assumed were for her and Chloe. Teegan's focus was on her tasks, but something didn't sit right with Kathleen. Teegan seemed a little off.

"Are you okay?"

Teegan glanced over her shoulder, as she leaned into the fridge to put the cheese and mayo away. "Yeah. I hate what's going on with Beth's ex. I hope the police find him soon."

"Me too. She's in there now going over it all with them." No sooner had they arrived when Beth called the police and gave the despatcher her brief history with Darren and told about the vandalism at her sitter's house. Two uniformed officers had arrived twenty minutes later. Kathleen was surprised at their quick response, but she supposed, with a potential murderer on the loose, they didn't want to take any chances. "I don't think she wants me to hear all the details." When the officers had asked about the night of the attack, Beth had turned wounded eyes toward Kathleen and asked her for some privacy. It hurt, knowing that Beth didn't want her with her as she recapped the event. She tried to understand how difficult it was for Beth to relive that time in her life.

"She's trying to protect you," Teegan said, coming to stand in front of Kathleen where she leaned against the island.

"From what? I already know what happened."

137

Teegan chuckled and shook her head. "Are you seriously this clueless about women?" She waved her hand dismissively, not giving Kathleen a chance to respond. "Never mind, I can see that you are." She folded her arms. "Let me ask you this. When you first learned of what happened to her, what did you do?"

"I avoided her." Not her finest moment, and she hated to admit it now.

"Why?"

"At first I thought it was because I couldn't handle it, but deep down, I didn't like to see her hurt."

"You felt sorry for her," Teegan surmised and nodded.

"Yeah."

"That's why she sent you out. She doesn't want your sympathy. She wants you to love her for who she is, not for what she's been through." She ducked her head, catching Kathleen's gaze. "Make sense?"

"She needs to feel like an equal partner, not a victim."

"Exactly."

"How did you get so smart?" Kathleen grinned.

"I may not have liked the therapy I was forced into when I went into foster care, but I did learn a thing or two." Just then, Teegan's mobile vibrated across the island. Teegan glanced at the caller ID and sighed, hitting decline. It wasn't hard to see the displeasure in her features.

"Who keeps calling?"

"It's Shane. He's been ringing and texting for a couple of days now. I told him I don't want to see him, but he keeps on bugging me."

"Have you blocked the number?" Kathleen had wondered how long it would be until he made an appearance. She hoped Teegan wouldn't be swayed into seeing him. He was a low life, and she'd be damned if he got his claws back into Teegan.

"Yeah, he just uses a friend's phone or buys a new SIM card." Teegan glanced at the phone again, then reached for it. "You know what? Let's make it easier for me for a change." She took the phone out of its case and removed the back cover. She slid the SIM card out and snapped it in two. "I'll get a new card at some point." She tossed the broken bits in the bin.

"What about your social media and messaging apps?"

"He's blocked from all my accounts, and I don't accept requests I don't know. Eventually, he'll give up."

Kathleen hoped that was true. With all the crap going on right now with Beth's ex, the last thing they needed was Shane turning up. Changing the subject, she asked, "Did you get Chloe settled?"

"She's up in my room trying to find something on Netflix for us to watch. She didn't want to stay by herself, so I offered to let her stay with me."

"You get on really well with her."

Teegan went to the fridge again, taking out two cans of Coke and stuffing them into her pockets. "For a kid, she's pretty cool. I never had any siblings, so it's kinda nice to hang around with her, you know, pass on my life experience." She grinned then picked up the plates.

"She's thirteen. She doesn't need to know *that* much," Kathleen said with a grin.

"Don't worry, I won't corrupt her." Teegan winked and began to walk out of the room. She hesitated and turned around. "Kath?"

"Yeah?"

"You're a good person. We're lucky we have you looking out for us."

That brought a smile to her lips and a slight blush to her cheeks. "Thanks. Good night."

"See ya."

Kathleen pulled out a barstool and sat. She laid her head on her arms on the island's cool surface. Friday afternoon she wasn't sure inviting Teegan to stay was a good idea, but it had turned out to be a blessing. She was a good kid, just as Kathleen suspected, and had proved herself trustworthy. She really had done an amazing job driving Beth and Chloe back there. Kathleen's thoughts turned to the conversation in the other room. She had to fight her instinct to go to Beth, forcing herself to remain in the kitchen. It was killing her, not being able to support Beth through this. She felt comforted by Teegan's words, about Beth wanting to protect her. The thought made her smile. She had never thought she would need anyone. The way she had treated Meredith had convinced her she wasn't worth loving. Beth had changed all that. She had opened a door within Kathleen, a door to the possibility of happiness. She wanted to walk through that door with Beth, but in order to do that Beth would have to stay. And Darren would need to disappear.

"Hi."

Beth's voice from behind startled her from her musings. She swivelled on the stool to face her. "Have they gone?" She held out her hand for Beth to take, which she did eagerly. Kathleen tugged her closer then looped her arms around her waist. Beth's hands settled on Kathleen's thighs.

"Yes."

"How are you feeling?" Kathleen's gaze roamed over Beth's lovely face. She noted the dark skin under her eyes and the fine lines at her temples that seemed to have taken up residence in the last few hours. *She looks worn out.* At that moment, all Kathleen wanted to do was take Beth upstairs and tuck her into bed, holding her close and keeping her safe.

"Still pretty rattled," Beth answered. "They wanted to know everything. They're going to put out an alert, but unless he shows up, there isn't much they can do. I still think leaving is the best option."

"You can't go until your friend sorts out the documents you need. Until then, it's best to stay put."

Beth's eyes narrowed. "You're not going to argue with me about this?"

"No." Kathleen leaned forward and pecked her on the lips, pulling back with a grin. "I'm hoping they find Darren before your friend is done with your paperwork. Then maybe you'll stay."

Beth smiled. She turned serious, running her fingertips lightly over Kathleen's denim-covered thighs. "I don't know how I would have managed tonight without you. Thank you."

"No thanks needed." Kathleen was just glad that Teegan had insisted they go over to Beth's after work. Originally, she had planned to go home and let Beth contact her if she wanted to, wanting her to have space. Now, she didn't want to be anywhere but with Beth.

"Did you mean what you said, about loving me?" There was a slight hesitation in her voice.

"Yes," Kathleen answered immediately. "I know it's too soon or whatever, but from the moment I saw you with soup splattered all over yourself, I began to fall. It's gotten stronger every day."

Beth stared at her for a moment. "I love you too. But you know it won't work, don't you? We have to leave."

"We'll see."

Kathleen didn't want to think about Beth not ever being in her life. She didn't like the hollow feeling that settled in her chest every time the thought showed up. She had been alone for most of her life. Even during the four years with Meredith, she had never been completely with her. She always kept her emotional distance. It wasn't like that with Beth. Beth filled her in ways she never thought possible.

"Is Chloe in bed?"

"She's up in Teegan's room."

"She reminds me of you."

"Teegan?" Kathleen's head lurched back.

"Yeah. Strong, brave, beautiful."

Kathleen completely agreed that Teegan was all those things. As she got older, she would be stunning, and she had the heart of a lioness. But herself? No, she barely knew what she was doing day to day. Wasn't that why she was on sabbatical in the first place? Because she was weak. "I don't think I'm any of those things."

"Oh, you are." Beth caressed her cheek and kissed her. "You just don't realise it."

Kathleen shook her head. She had no idea what Beth saw in her. For much of her life, it had always been about business, making sure she was the best at what she did. Not until meeting Beth did she begin to realise there was more to her own personality than just work. Now she was talking of love and inviting teenagers to come to live with her.

"What do you want to do about the centre?" she asked, wanting to change the uncomfortable subject. There was only so much self-discovery she could handle at a time.

"If you can still sort security, I'd like to go in. It's probably not a good idea, but I can't sit here waiting for him to show up." Her eyes sparkled. "If you're determined not to let me leave yet, I'd like to continue working."

Kathleen felt a wave of guilt wash over her. She didn't want Beth thinking she was trying to control her. "You know you can leave if you want to, right? I don't want to be the one standing in the way if that's what you really want."

"It's true, I want to be as far away from Darren as I possibly can. However, the thought of leaving you is too painful. I want to stay with you for as long as possible."

"I want that too." Kathleen pulled her in close and held her tightly.

"I want you to know something," Beth whispered into her shoulder. "My name is Hannah Kirkdale. Chloe's real name is Zoe." She leaned back in Kathleen's embrace. "I chose Chloe for her because it rhymes. She was young, and I figured it would be easier for her to remember. If she slipped up, people would think she just mispronounced it."

"Smart thinking." *Hannah.* She gazed at Beth saying the name over in her head. She didn't look like a Hannah. "Hannah." She said the name aloud, testing the word on her lips. It sounded okay, but Beth sounded better. "It has a nice ring to it."

"I prefer Beth. I like who I am with that name."

I do too. "Well, we need to make sure you won't have to go changing it again."

"I'm still leaving," Beth warned, the glint still in her eye.

"We'll see," Kathleen replied, pulling her in for another kiss. "Are you hungry?"

"Not really. I want to check on Chloe and then lie down, maybe watch some tele before I fall asleep."

143

Kathleen stood from the stool, still holding Beth's hand. "I'll show you to your room." Beth tugged on her hand and stopped her from moving.

"I was kinda hoping I could stay with you if that's okay? I'll feel safer if you're next to me."

"Sounds perfect."

CHAPTER SIXTEEN

"Are you sure you still want to do this?" Kathleen stopped in the centre's carpark and pulled on the handbrake. Beth's eyes scanned the rear of the building, then behind the car. Though her fear was palpable, Kathleen could also see the determination in her eyes.

"Did you manage to sort out security?"

"Yes. Maggie called while you were in the shower. She arrived about an hour ago. She's checked the perimeter, and nothing seemed out of place. She should be waiting out front, ready to let us in. She'll check the building before we enter."

The hands that clutched Beth's thighs relaxed when Kathleen laid hers on top. "Everything will be fine. Teegan and Chloe are going to help Francine in the kitchen, then hang out in the dayroom. Maggie is really good at her job. She won't let anybody in without your say so."

"Okay." After taking a deep breath, Beth grabbed her door handle. "Let's go."

They all stepped from the car. Beth took Chloe's hand, and Kathleen and Teegan flanked them as they headed toward the main entrance. As Kathleen had said, Maggie was waiting for them by the front door. Easily topping six feet, she was an imposing figure. Her back was wide, and the muscles in her thighs were clearly visible through her blue jeans. If Darren did show up, he would need a gun to get past her.

An injury had ended Maggie's blossoming career in the army. Now she worked private security and was good at it. She had been hired to protect a high-profile politician, who wanted to change his investments. Kathleen and Maggie had become friendly through those client meetings, and there was no one else Kathleen trusted to keep Beth and Chloe safe. It also wouldn't hurt matters to have her around the centre, discouraging any trouble that might start from abusive partners and the like.

Kathleen shook Maggie's hand with a firm grip. "Maggie, thanks for this."

"No problem. I was between jobs anyway." Her gaze roamed over the group and Kathleen made introductions. "This is Beth, her daughter Chloe, and our friend Teegan."

"Nice to meet you all." She looked at Beth. "Did you bring a photo of your ex?"

"Yes." Beth reached into her bag and held out a photograph. "It's a little old, but it's all I have left." They had driven back to Beth's house that morning to retrieve it.

"This is fine. I'll be stopping anyone coming in anyway, unless you clear them. This will just help me get a general idea of what to look for." She stuffed the picture into her pocket. "If you let me in, I'll check inside." Beth did as requested, then stepped back. She wrapped her arms around Chloe. "This won't take long."

They waited outside, while Maggie disappeared through the door. Kathleen kept her gaze fixed on the surrounding area, checking faces of the early morning commuters and looking for anyone or anything that seemed out of place. After ten minutes, Maggie reappeared.

"All clear."

Maggie stepped aside so they could enter. Beth and Chloe went first. Kathleen held Teegan back. "What?" her eyebrows raised in question.

"I want you to give Shane's description to Maggie."

"What? Why?"

"Just in case." She didn't want to let on just how worried she was about Teegan. From what she had witnessed, he was an asshole. She wanted to make sure Teegan would be safe there. Kathleen couldn't be worrying about Beth *and* Teegan. It was too much. She also had a job to focus on. If she could make sure Shane stayed away, then she would have one less thing to worry about.

"Who's Shane?"

"My boyfriend, well ex-boyfriend." She pulled her phone from her pocket and began scrolling. "He's a little bit handsy."

"He's hit you?" Maggie's voice filled with venom. "You're a kid."

"I'm seventeen, hardly a child."

"But still, you're a little young to be beaten on."

147

"Violence can happen at any age." Teegan handed her phone over to Maggie. "He's an addict and can't control his anger. He's out of my life now."

Kathleen watched the exchange with mild fascination. She could clearly see the defiance in Teegan at being called a kid, and Maggie looked so furious a girl of Teegan's age could be caught up in domestic violence. They glared at each other for a moment, then smiled at the same time. The blush tinging Maggie's cheeks was cute, considering she was as butch as they come.

"Sorry, you're right." Maggie handed back the phone. "I'll keep an eye out for him."

"Thank you." Teegan's own cheeks heated under Maggie's gaze.

"Right," Kathleen said. "Let's get to work."

The day wore on, and no drama unfolded. If not for the fact Maggie was there, Kathleen could swear it was a normal day. No one questioned why Beth's daughter wasn't in school, and they all seemed thrilled and more relaxed to have a security guard on the premises. Kathleen idly wondered if she could keep Maggie on full time, once the business with Darren was over. It made sense to have her there, and she got on well with the clients. Kathleen laughed when she remembered Francine flirting with Maggie when she'd come in to grab a sandwich from the kitchen. Maggie played up to it and for a few minutes. Beth's face had relaxed with joy and laughter as Maggie was forced to waltz with Francine in her arms.

The end of the day arrived, and the place was cleaned up. After the staff and women left, Maggie walked them to Kathleen's car. There was no sign of Darren.

A voice sounded from the back of the carpark, just as they reached the car.

"Teegan."

Kathleen turned in time to see a scrawny teenage boy with greasy hair come running toward them. *Shane.* Before she had a chance to react, Maggie had stepped in front of Teegan and caught him around the waist. She grabbed his arm and twisted it up behind his back, then forcing him to the ground. She planted her knee between his shoulder blades, and Shane grunted from the force.

"What the fuck," he screamed.

Kathleen tried to hold Teegan back, but she pulled away, dropping to her knees next to Shane.

"I told you to leave me alone," Teegan seethed.

"I just want to talk. I'm sorry." He grunted again, as Maggie applied more pressure.

"If you don't leave me alone, my girlfriend here will snap you in two."

Kathleen refrained from laughing. The situation wasn't funny, but the look on his face when he thought the woman holding him down was Teegan's lover, that was priceless.

"You're not a dyke. Ow, shit. Stop it. You're hurting me."

Maggie leaned down and said, "It's less than what you deserve. Stay away or I'll make good on her promise."

"Okay, okay."

Maggie eased up the pressure, eventually letting him go. Shane shot to his feet and tried to lunge for Teegan again. A quick punch from Maggie dropped him to his knees, blood spurting out of his nose.

"Everyone get in the car," Maggie shouted.

Kathleen unlocked the doors and ushered Beth and Chloe inside the back seat. "Teegan, let's go." Teegan glanced at her then back to Shane, still on his knees and crying in pain.

"Hang on," she said to Kathleen. She stepped closer to him. "You're a pathetic mess. You come near me again and I'll have you arrested, that's if Maggie doesn't kill you first." She turned her back on him and got into the passenger side of the car, slamming the door.

Shane stumbled to his feet. For a moment, Kathleen thought he would try again to get to Teegan. He looked up at Maggie, then shook his head. He turned and sprinted away. Kathleen let out a relieved breath, hoping that was the last they would see of Shane. Maggie went to Teegan's window, which Teegan wound down.

"You okay?"

"Yes, thank you. I'm sorry for calling you my girlfriend. I just figured if he thought I was with you he might think twice about coming back."

Maggie grinned. "No problem. I think it worked." She winked at Teegan and said her goodbyes, strutting off back toward the centre.

"I think you just made her day," Beth said from the back seat.

Teegan's blush was adorable.

"How old is she anyway?" Beth asked Kathleen.

"Twenty-three."

"Huh," Teegan said.

Kathleen started the car and pulled away, thinking Teegan might just have the littlest of crushes on her new knight in shining armour.

†

The next few days went pretty much the same way, excluding Shane. Maggie met them at the front entrance and did her sweep of the building before letting them enter. The shy glances Teegan directed at Maggie worried Kathleen. She wasn't a prude, but she had assumed Teegan was straight. Teegan had also been through a hell of a lot in her short life. Kathleen didn't want her getting her heart broken again. Teegan needed time to sort herself out before jumping into anything. Kathleen wondered if maybe she should have a word with Maggie, asking her to not encourage Teegan's crush. Really though, it was none of her business. She wasn't Teegan's mother. She would sit back and let things develop however they did. If she thought there might be trouble, then she would say something. She didn't want to alienate Teegan so soon.

The day had been uneventful and for that Kathleen was grateful. Everyone had still been on edge when they arrived at Kathleen's home Tuesday evening. Chloe was a little freaked out by having seen Shane bleeding and going after Teegan. Beth had managed to calm her daughter, but it was Teegan who worried Kathleen the most. After Chloe was settled for the night, Teegan burst into tears. Kathleen was so shocked, she had no clue as to what to do. It was Beth who comforted Teegan, telling her it wasn't her fault and that she was brave to stand up to him. Teegan went to bed feeling better and actually seemed to wake up feeling happy.

Kathleen and Beth had been sharing the master bed, and Kathleen relished holding her all night. It was an act she was becoming addicted to, even after only two nights together. Her libido was being tested. She had never spent the night just holding someone. She usually only stayed over with Meredith when they had sex. Otherwise, she would always go home after their date. This intimacy was a new experience, but she found she loved it. If they never made love, Kathleen would be content to just hold her.

Nearing six o'clock, Kathleen was so lost in her thoughts of Beth that she didn't notice Meredith standing in front of her desk until she cleared her throat. Kathleen blinked and shook her head, not sure she hadn't conjured Meredith by thinking of her a moment ago.

"Hey," Kathleen said. "What are you doing here?"

"I arrived early for the group tonight, thought we could catch up."

"Have a seat." Kathleen gestured to the guest chair, her stomach twisting. The feelings of guilt she associated with Meredith were still present. She doubted they would ever leave. "How are the wedding plans going?"

Meredith's face lit up. Her obvious joy at marrying the love of her life made her usually beautiful features look radiant. A stab of jealousy hit Kathleen. She pushed it aside. Meredith deserved to be happy. Kathleen would never have been able to bring that joy to Meredith, so she was pleased Stephanie could.

"That good, huh?"

"I can't wait." Meredith caught Kathleen's gaze. "You're still invited, don't forget."

Kathleen shook her head. "I really don't think Stephanie—"

"I already asked her. She's fine with it. I think she probably wants to rub it in your face." Meredith smiled to take the sting out of her words. "She thinks you're an idiot." Her smile grew wider.

"She would be correct in that assessment." Kathleen leaned forward, smiling. "I am really happy for you both. I'm just sorry I–"

"Don't you dare apologise again, or I'll be forced to smack you upside the head."

"Okay." Kathleen grinned, knowing full well Meredith wouldn't hurt a bug.

"How's it going here? I'm glad you've stuck it out."

"It's been a challenge. The accounts are still frozen, so we're running on limited funds. Beth has been amazing at changing things around and making sure the clients still get the help they need."

"Oh jeez."

"What?" Kathleen drew her eyebrows down, confused. Whatever she had just said had caused Meredith to grimace and shake her head imperceptibly.

Meredith waved her hand. "It's nothing."

"Mere, just tell me."

Taking a breath, Meredith said, "When you spoke about Beth, your eyes got all dreamy. Your cheeks flushed and you formed the most honest smile I've ever seen on you. You've fallen for her, haven't you?"

Kathleen thought about denying the accusation, but she found she couldn't make the words come out. She nodded. "Yes." Meredith closed her eyes briefly, obviously not pleased with her answer.

"You have no idea what's she's been through." Anger marred Meredith's tone. "You were supposed to come here to work, not hit on the staff."

Kathleen's temper flared. She couldn't believe what she was hearing. "How dare you assume you know anything that's between us."

"You've slept with her." It wasn't a question.

"What? No. Not that it's any of your business. A lot has happened in the last few weeks. We've talked. I like her, a lot." Kathleen wanted to tell Meredith everything, to make her understand the depth of her feelings, but it really was none of her business. She also didn't want to divulge Beth's personal business without her consent. "I've never felt this way before."

"Damn. You're right, you haven't. I can see it all over your face. You're in love, aren't you?"

Kathleen looked down at her desk. Guilt crept up again. She had never loved Meredith the way she deserved. "I'm sorry, but yeah, I am."

They sat staring at each other for a few moments, neither speaking. Finally, Meredith asked, "Does she feel the same?"

Kathleen nodded.

"Well, in that case, you can bring her as your plus one to the wedding."

"What?" That was the last thing she expected Meredith to say. She thought Meredith would give her more grief.

"I can't pretend to understand. She was married to a man, not that it would be the first time a woman has come to terms with her sexuality. I just didn't think she would..."

"Be in love with someone like me." Kathleen finished for her. Before Meredith could refute the statement, she continued, "You're right. I didn't think it would be possible either. But I'm not the same woman I was a year ago. After we broke up, I sunk into this deep sadness. I felt empty all the time. I'd treated you so badly that I hated myself. When you offered me up to work here, I couldn't see what that would achieve. But I feel at peace here. Helping these women and children has filled a hole in me I didn't know needed filling. And Beth, she's amazing. She's so strong and capable. She doesn't take any of my shit. I can't explain it. I feel connected to her."

"I'm happy you're finally seeing yourself in a better light. That's all I want for you. And for you to be happy. To forgive yourself."

"I'm a long way from doing that, but with Beth, I know I have a chance to redeem myself. She makes me want to change."

A loud boom sounded from the back of the building, then the fire alarms went off.

CHAPTER SEVENTEEN

Kathleen shot to her feet. She grabbed Meredith's hand and ran out of the office. She could hear shouts coming from the main hall, panicked voices yelling to get out. She shouldered through the hall door, Meredith behind her. Smoke was filling the room from the direction of the kitchen. She frantically searched for Beth in the midst of women charging toward the main entrance. She turned to Meredith. "Go. Get out and call the fire brigade. I'm going to make sure everyone is out." She didn't give Meredith a chance to argue. Kathleen turned on her heel and ran toward the kitchen.

She peered through the glass window in the door. Flames engulfed every surface, and black smoke leaked through the edges of the door frame. She couldn't see anyone in there, so she turned back around. She spotted Maggie by the door to the foyer, guiding people out. Reaching her, she asked, "Where's Beth and Chloe?"

"Chloe is outside with Teegan. Beth went upstairs to check the offices and the night room."

Fear overtook Kathleen. The night room was directly above the kitchen. With the amount of fire in there, it wouldn't take long for it to burn through the ceiling to where Beth was. She glanced at Maggie. "Make sure everyone here gets out. I'm going to find Beth."

Maggie grabbed her. "That's crazy. No sense in both of you going up there."

"I'm not leaving her here." She shook Maggie's hand off and sprinted away. The stairway was already filling with smoke. She pulled her shirt up over her nose and mouth to help her breathe through the smog, but the smoke still burned her eyes. She reached the landing and called Beth's name, not hearing a reply. As she progressed down the hall, she checked the offices and storage cupboards, pleased they were all empty. She got to the night room door and pushed it open. As she did so, the floor gave way and dropped into the kitchen below. Mortified, she stepped back, Beth's name stuck in her throat. She wanted to call out, but no sound emerged. She had a terrible feeling Beth had gone through the floor with the beds and end tables.

She couldn't move. She had lost everything. Her hand fell limply to her side, her shirt no longer covering her mouth. The tears that ran down her face now were not made by the smoke but at the loss of her soul. She sunk to her knees and wept, not caring that flames were licking up the walls of the night room and moving toward her.

†

"Maggie," Beth called out.

Maggie whipped around. "I thought you were upstairs?"

"I was. It's all clear. We have to get out of here now. The place is empty." Beth held Maggie's hand as they exited. She was pleased when sirens could be heard in the distance. She had no idea what had happened. One minute she was setting up chairs, and the next, the place had gone up in flames. She was just thankful that everyone had been in the main hall and had managed to escape.

"Did Kathleen find you then?" Maggie asked, as they crossed the road to the safest distance away from the fire.

Beth shook her head, confused. "What are you talking about? I assumed she was out here with everyone else."

"No. She went upstairs to look for you."

A loud crash sounded from the building. Beth's let out a blood curdling "No". Her legs were moving before she could stop them, but she didn't get far. Maggie's strong arms came around her waist and held her back.

"You can't go in there. The whole place is coming down."

Beth turned wild eyes onto Maggie. "She's still in there. We have to find her."

"Who?"

She glanced over her shoulder. Meredith was standing behind her with Chloe and Teegan in tow. "Kath." She stumbled over the words then found herself engulfed in Meredith's arms. She slumped into her, clinging to her with all her strength.

"No fucking way," Teegan said angrily. She sprinted toward the main entrance.

"Teegan, no," Beth shouted, but Teegan didn't stop running. She disappeared through the smoke. Maggie took a step forward, but Beth halted her with a tug on her arm. "We all stay here. The fire brigade is here now."

Maggie looked like she wanted to refuse. "I'll go tell them we have two still inside."

Beth watched her walk away, then turned to Meredith. "What if she's dead? What am I going to do?"

Meredith pulled her into another hug. "She's too stubborn to let anything happen to her. She'll be fine."

Beth hoped that was true. Any other possibility just wouldn't do. She felt Chloe take her hand and Beth pulled her into the shelter of Meredith's arms along with her. All eyes were focused on the building that was once their safe haven.

Beth's stomach clenched repeatedly, as she watched the firefighters enter the building. Her gaze stayed on the entrance, praying with everything in her that Kathleen and Teegan would emerge safely. Minutes passed.

Movement by the door caught her attention. Teegan stumbled out, her hands under Kathleen's arms. A fireman had hold of her feet. They laid her on the ground, and the fireman began CPR. Beth let go of Chloe's hand and ran to Kathleen. She nudged Teegan out of the way. Coughing repeatedly, Teegan sank to her knees at Kathleen's head. Kathleen's clothes and face were covered with soot, the sleeve of her right arm was burned away, the skin mottled with blisters. Beth grabbed Kathleen's left hand and squeezed her fingers. The fireman worked steadily for a few minutes. Beth watched and waited anxiously.

Kathleen coughed once, then twice. Her eyes flickered open for just a moment. Another fireman secured an oxygen mask on her face, then made way for an ambulance crew who had just arrived on the scene.

"Excuse me, ma'am. We need some room," one of them said.

Beth stood on shaky legs and watched as they ran a line into Kathleen's left arm and placed a dressing over her right. They lifted her onto a stretcher and wheeled her into the ambulance. In a matter of moments, Kathleen was gone. Beth felt a hand touch her back. It was Maggie.

"My truck is parked up the road. I'll take you and Teegan to the hospital."

Beth nodded, still unable to speak. Kathleen was alive, that was all that mattered. She turned her gaze to search out Chloe, finding her next to Teegan, wiping soot off Teegan's face.

"Let's go get you checked out." She held her hands out for Chloe and Teegan to take.

"I'll meet you there," Meredith said.

Beth smiled. "Thanks." They followed Maggie to her truck and set off for the hospital. *She has to be all right.*

CHAPTER EIGHTEEN

"Any news," Teegan asked, as Beth stepped into her cubicle. Teegan was sitting on a bed, a blue gown draped around her torso. She had an oxygen mask held loosely in her grasp, not where Beth thought it should be.

"Shouldn't you be wearing that?" She pointed to the device.

Teegan shrugged. "The air makes my throat hurt."

"I imagine that's the damage the smoke caused." She reached out and slid the mask back over Teegan's mouth and nose. "I'll talk, you just concentrate on breathing." She waited until she was sure Teegan wouldn't remove the mask again. "Kath is being put up in a room for monitoring. Her CO levels were dangerously high, so they want to keep an eye on her. A plastic surgeon is coming down to take a look at her arm. The doctor doesn't think it's too serious, but she might have a few scars. She was extremely lucky."

Once they had arrived at the hospital, Beth immediately got someone to look at Teegan. Meredith and Maggie took Chloe to the onsite café, keeping her secluded from the drama of the emergency room. When everyone was sorted, Beth had searched out information on Kathleen. She lied to the receptionist, saying Kathleen was her wife, so they would give her an update. She knew hospital policy was to share information only with relatives, but Beth had no idea about any of Kathleen's family. The thought of not knowing what was going on with Kathleen didn't bare thinking about. The receptionist and doctor she spoke to didn't even ask for any form of ID. *So much for hospital security.* She idly wondered at the state of the health care system.

"That was an incredibly stupid thing you did back there," Beth said. "You could have gotten yourself killed." Teegan looked down at her lap, lips frowning. Beth gently raised Teegan's chin and looked directly in her eyes. "I am very thankful you were stupid. You saved her life."

Teegan's eyes filled with tears that rolled down her cheeks and around the mask. "I didn't think. I just had to find her." Her voice was muffled by the plastic mask.

Beth smiled. "I know. Thank you." She leaned forward and kissed Teegan's forehead. "Can you tell me what happened?"

Teegan reached up and pulled the mask off, ignoring Beth's pointed stare and shake of her head. "Maggie said Kath had gone upstairs to find you, so that's where I headed." Her voice came out husky, and she had to keep clearing her throat as she spoke. "The whole place was thick with smoke. I kept as low as I could and went upstairs. She was lying at the end of the hallway, her arm hanging through the doorway to the night room." More tears fell, and she reached up to wipe them away. "I thought she was dead. I didn't try and wake her. I just grabbed her arms and pulled as hard as I could. I got her halfway down the stairs, when I saw a fireman coming up. He helped me get her out."

Beth settled her weight next to Teegan and put the mask back in place. "You're a very brave young woman. I can't tell you how much I'm thankful you were there today."

Teegan shrugged. "She would have done the same for me." Teegan was right about that. The Kathleen Beth was coming to know would have moved mountains to get back into that building to save someone. Beth still didn't understand why Kathleen thought herself so worthless. Kathleen had more than proved how compassionate, caring, and loving she was. Beth just hoped Kathleen would realise it herself, and soon.

"If I go see her, can I trust you to keep that on?" Beth indicated the mask again. Teegan grinned and nodded. "Okay. I'll see you soon." She settled the curtain back into place as she left.

One floor up, she found Kathleen's room. She looked through the glass, and a wave of jealousy swamped her. Meredith was sitting next to the bed, her hand clutching Kathleen's. It was an irrational emotion. Meredith was happily in love with her partner, but that didn't erase the history the two of them had shared. They had both admitted their relationship wasn't as serious, or as deep, as they'd thought at the time. Still, they'd had four years together. It had been clear they held feelings for each other. However, Beth knew they were feelings of friendship, as tentative as that friendship was at the moment.

Beth shook her jealousy aside and stepped into the room. Meredith glanced up and smiled. She let go of Kathleen's hand and came around the bed to hug Beth.

"How is Teegan?" Meredith asked.

"She's fine. Her throat is a little sore and her lungs took a kicking, but she'll be good as new—as long as she keeps the oxygen mask on." Beth gazed at Kathleen's still form under the blanket. The soot had been washed away from her face but still lingered in her hair. Her arm was fully bandaged, and IV drips hung from a stand next to the bed. A steady beep tracked her heartbeat and comforted Beth. Without warning, tears sprang from her eyes.

"She's going to be fine." Meredith took her hand.

"I know. But she came so close."

"Here, sit down. I left Maggie with Chloe in the canteen." Meredith tugged Beth's hand and guided her into the vacated chair. "It's serious between you two, isn't it?"

Beth glanced away from Kathleen's face into Meredith's eyes. She nodded. "We didn't start off great, but the last few weeks, with everything going on with my ex, she's been amazing."

"Your ex?"

Beth sighed. Meredith knew about Darren but didn't know the full story. She didn't know Beth had been in hiding with an assumed name. She didn't know Darren was stalking her, or that she had moved into Kathleen's place. Beth decided to lay it all out for her. Twenty minutes later…

"Bloody hell, that's a lot to take in," Meredith said.

"It hasn't been easy. I've contacted the friend who got me my identity last time, to fix me up again. I was hoping to be gone in a couple of weeks."

"What about Kath?"

"She understands it's my decision. Although, she's hoping the police will find him before I leave."

Meredith was silent for a moment, the skin around her eyes creasing as she thought. "If all you've told me about what's happened is Darren's doing, do you think he could have been responsible for the fire?"

Beth didn't need to ponder the question. It had already crossed her mind. "My guess is yes, but it could also be a number of other things. Accidental, any other woman's partner who might want revenge against the centre, Shane."

"Who's Shane?"

"Teegan's old boyfriend. He's been hitting her and turned up last night to see her. He didn't like it when Maggie put him on the ground with a bloody nose."

"So, it really could be anyone."

"Yeah. The police will have to look into all this. My main concern now is keeping my family safe." Her gaze drifted back to Kathleen, knowing her family meant Kathleen too. A tall, dark-haired woman strolled through the door. The newcomer went to Meredith and swept her up into a fierce hug.

"Are you okay?" the newcomer whispered into Meredith's ear.

"I'm fine, darling." Meredith pulled back and made introductions. "Beth, this is my fiancée, Stephanie. Steph, meet Beth. She runs the centre."

Beth held out her hand, mesmerised by Stephanie's intense, dark eyes. *No wonder Meredith fell in love with her. She's gorgeous.* They shook hands then turned their attention to the patient.

"How is she?" Stephanie asked.

"She's going to be fine," Beth said. "She's too stubborn to let this keep her down."

Stephanie grinned. "Yeah, she is. I also like to use the word idiot a lot to describe her."

"I'm not dead yet. I can still hear you," came Kathleen's quiet reply.

"Oh my God, Kath?" Beth leaned over the bed and gazed into the most perfect blue eyes she had ever known. "I'm so glad you're awake. I was so scared."

"I thought you were gone," Kathleen murmured, tears filling her eyes.

"No. Never." She quickly kissed her on the lips, not caring what other people were in the room. She pulled back and allowed her hand to move into Kathleen's hair, ignoring the soot that now transferred onto her hand. "Don't you ever worry me like that again."

"I promise." Kathleen's gaze drifted to Meredith and Stephanie. "Did everyone get out okay?"

"All present and accounted for," Meredith answered.

"Good." Her eyes closed for a second then popped open. "Teegan. I thought I heard Teegan calling for me."

"You did," Beth said. "She went back in to get you."

"Damn idiot," Kathleen said, grinning.

Stephanie cleared her throat. "Seems a lot like you." Though the words sounded mean, Stephanie wore a gentle smile.

"Honey," Meredith admonished. "Play nice."

"She knows it's true."

"Yeah, I do."

Kathleen's eyes closed again, and Beth could see her struggling to stay awake. She turned to Meredith. "I don't want to leave her here on her own. Do you think you could

166

look after Chloe and Teegan?" She was loath to leave her daughter, but there was no way she could walk out of the hospital without Kathleen. She didn't like having to ask for help. She trusted Meredith to look after Chloe.

"Of course," Stephanie replied. "We'll get a movie and pizza. I can put an air bed up in my studio, and we have the couch. Plenty of room."

"Thank you. I'll call you when I know what's happening with Kath."

"There's no hurry. We'll be fine." Meredith hugged her.

Beth was still concerned Darren could be watching. "Could you be careful leaving? Just in case Darren is hanging about."

"We'll be fine," Meredith repeated. "Don't worry."

"Okay. Thank you."

Beth glanced back at Kathleen, then went to find Chloe. The anguish and adrenalin over nearly losing Kathleen still pumped through her veins. When the effects finally wore off, she would be dead on her feet. All she wanted was to go home and lay snuggled up in Kathleen's arms. Hopefully, Kathleen wouldn't have to be admitted for too long.

CHAPTER NINETEEN

Kathleen became fully awake when a blinding pain shot through her right arm. Groaning, she clenched her fist and waited for the agony to subside. Her breaths came short and fast, and she could feel her pulse pounding through her arm in time to the pain. She felt cool fingers touch her forehead, then smooth her hair back. The touch soothed her, and a moment later the throbbing diminished, although she could still feel it. She opened her eyes, noting the hospital room was coated in a muted glow. Turning her head to the side, a welcome sight greeted her. Beth leaned over, her face marred with worry.

"Hey, babe," Kathleen croaked.

"Hi. Do you want me to get the nurse to give you some pain relief?"

"No, it's okay, now you're here." Kathleen raised her left hand for Beth to take. The debilitating fear she felt when she thought Beth had died still lingered. Seeing Beth before her now was the greatest gift she had ever received. Tears fell from her eyes, and Beth smiled tenderly as she wiped them away.

"I was so scared you were gone. I never want you to leave me." Kathleen hated sounding so weak, but she needed Beth to know how much she loved her. Beth looked away, her lips set tight. Kathleen's pulse kicked up again. "What's going on?" She wasn't sure she wanted to know. When Beth looked back at her, Kathleen knew their time was up. Her heart snapped like a dry twig. "What is it?"

"The police came by earlier to talk to me. They found Darren's fingerprints at the sitter's house." She stared at the wall. "There is evidence that the fire at the centre was set intentionally. Also, my house was broken into. A neighbour called the police when they heard noises coming from the back door. The police feel it's Darren. He's getting closer. It's only a matter of time before he finds me."

Kathleen tried hard to keep her breathing steady. As much as she wanted Beth to stay, her safety and Chloe's was more important. "When do you leave?" she asked in a whisper, stumbling over the words.

"You know I don't want to go, right?" Her eyes filled with tears.

"Yes."

"The centre was supposed to be a safe haven for women and children, a place to escape their pasts. I never thought it would be *my* past that took that away from them."

Kathleen reached up and cupped Beth's cheek. "This isn't your fault. None of it is."

169

Beth covered Kathleen's hand with her own, pressing her cheek more firmly into her warm fingers. "The doctor wants you to stay here for a few more days, then you can go home. I've spoken to Teegan. She'll look after you while you recover. Meredith says she'll help out too."

As much as Kathleen loved Teegan and Meredith, it wasn't them she wanted by her side, nursing her back to health. She supposed she deserved to have her heart broken, especially after the way she treated Meredith and her own mother, but she had no idea it would hurt this bad. "Will I ever see you again?" Beth turned away, her shoulders slumping. Her body shook as she cried. Kathleen reached out and touched her back. "Please don't cry. It'll be all right."

Beth spun away, her tears giving way to anger. "How can you say that? He's taking everything away from me, again. I had finally felt settled in my life. Chloe was doing well in school, and I found you. Why can't he just leave me alone?"

Kathleen had no answers. Life was cruel and unfair, and no amount of talking about it was going to change the facts. Beth needed to leave, and Kathleen had to let her go. "Call Maggie. I want her to take you where you need to go. She's good at what she does. She'll keep you safe."

There was a long pause before Beth nodded. "I will."

"Will you be able to contact me? Let me know where you are?"

"I don't know if that's a good idea. It'll just make things worse." Beth alluded to their separation. She was right, it was probably best to cut all ties, rather than drag out the inevitable.

"I love you, Beth."

"Oh God, I love you too."

Carefully pulling Beth closer, Kathleen kissed her with as much love as she could, knowing it would likely be the last time she would ever taste her, or even touch her. She savoured the moment, committing it to memory.

Beth pulled back and glanced at the clock. "The sun will be up soon. I need to collect Chloe and phone Maggie."

Kathleen closed her eyes for a breath and found her strength. She nodded. "Good luck, Beth. Be safe."

"Goodbye, Kath." She ran gentle fingers over Kathleen's cheek and left without looking back.

The door closed softly behind her. Kathleen lay in the dim light. The quiet of the room felt claustrophobic. She closed her eyes and tried to settle her racing heart. The pain of losing Beth was worse than any pain the fire had caused.

"No." Kathleen's eyelids popped open. What the hell was she doing? How could she just let her walk away? Kathleen's mind raced, as she tried to think of any plausible reason not to go after her. Kathleen had money. She could go with them and help keep them safe. Her job at the centre was now gone, and she didn't plan on going back to work for Gerard. There really were no ties keeping her from leaving Bristol with Beth. Did Beth want her to?

Sitting up made her dizzy. She pulled out the IV needle, wincing at the sharp pain. Blood trickled from the vein. She lifted the puncture site to her mouth, pressing her tongue hard to help stem the flow. She swung her legs over the side of the bed and stood. Pain exploded down her arm as gravity pulled blood through her right arm. She ignored it. Kathleen didn't care that she wore only a hospital gown. As fast as her feet could carry her, she left the room and went in search of Beth. She was sure Beth didn't have her car, as they had arrived to work in Kathleen's. Beth would either need to use a taxi or wait for Maggie to collect her. Ignoring the looks from the hospital staff as she hurried toward the lifts, she ran through her options. If Beth had called Maggie, she would wait for her inside. Otherwise, she would leave the hospital now and go to the taxi rank. Kathleen would head there first.

As the lift took her down to the ground floor, Kathleen leaned against the cab wall. Her head thumped and her stomach protested. There was a reason the doctors wanted her to stay in the hospital. She didn't care though. She had to find Beth before it was too late. The lift stopped and she stepped out, looking for the exit. The automatic doors whooshed open, and the cold morning air chilled her skin. Kathleen's nipples hardened beneath the thin gown. She spotted the taxi rank a hundred yards away. She scanned the area looking for Beth but couldn't see her. She was too late.

Beth was gone.

"Kath? What are you doing out here?"

Kathleen spun around. Beth stood there before her. Kathleen took a few steps forward and crushed Beth to her chest. "I can't let you go," she said in a panic.

"Honey, you can't be out here. You're not well."

"I don't care. I'm going with you." Kathleen pulled back. "Please, let me come with you."

Beth shook her head. "You need to be in hospital."

"I need to be with you." Kathleen waited through the silence, fearing she would be sent away.

"You can't give up your life for me, for a life on the run."

"I have no life without you. Please, Beth."

"This is crazy. You know that right?"

"Is that a yes?" She let Beth take her hand and hold it to her chest. She could feel Beth's heart pounding under her skin.

"You're in no fit state to be gallivanting around the country right now," Beth said. "We need to be somewhere Darren won't be able to find us. He might know where you live. If he's been watching us, he'll know I've been coming to work with you."

"I'll ask Meredith if we can stay with them for a few days."

Beth scanned the area around them. "We need to go. Now. I don't feel right being out in the open."

Kathleen looked down at herself, barefoot and in the hospital gown. It would have to do. Her clothes were removed when she arrived, and her belongings were now in a pile of smouldering ash. She took Beth's hand and led her the last few yards to the taxi rank. "Let's get out of here."

†

The taxi pulled up outside Meredith's apartment block twenty minutes later. Beth had called her to make sure it was okay to stay with them. Although Meredith wasn't happy Kathleen had left the hospital, she had agreed. Kathleen exited the taxi while Beth paid the driver. Her strength was fading fast, and the agony in her arm was causing her stomach to clench repeatedly. If she didn't lie down soon, there was a good chance she'd be flat on the pavement spewing up what little she had in her guts. Cool fingers slipped into her hand, giving it a squeeze.

"You okay?" Beth's worry wasn't hard to miss.

"I just need to lie down. I'm feeling queasy."

"Let's go then."

Together, they walked up the stone path to the main entrance and buzzed Meredith's number. The door released, and they made slow progress up the stairs to the fourth floor. The apartment block was essentially four flats stacked on top of each other, Meredith owned the top floor. They didn't need to knock. Meredith already had the door open.

"You guys realise this is a stupid idea, don't you? She should be in the hospital."

"I'm fine." Kathleen tried to smile through the pain. Meredith was right, it was a stupid idea. But the thought of going back to the hospital without Beth panicked her. Beth could disappear from her life altogether, and that was something Kathleen wouldn't be able to live with. "My arm will take a few days to heal, but it isn't serious. Stop fussing."

Meredith shook her head and stepped back from the threshold to allow them to enter. Beth's arm wound around Kathleen's waist, and she tried not to lean on her too much. She wanted to give the impression she was stronger than what she was actually feeling. As they entered the lounge, Kathleen cast her gaze around. Not much had changed in the year since she had last been there, except she could see more of Stephanie's presence in the room. Beth led her to the sofa and helped her sit down. Kathleen grunted as she sat, grateful that the room had stopped spinning. She looked up at Meredith.

"I'm sorry it's so early," Kathleen said.

"It's fine. Teegan and Chloe are still asleep in Steph's studio. Steph is changing the sheets in our room, so you two can stay in there. We'll pop out later and get another air bed for us to use in the lounge tonight."

"Um, Mere," Kathleen said, "As much as I'm grateful for everything you're doing, I don't think it's a good idea for me to use your bed."

174

"Why?" Meredith's eyebrows pinched together.

"It, um, would be a little weird." No way did Kathleen want to sleep in the same bed she once shared with Meredith, a bed Meredith now shared with Stephanie. A little weird was an understatement.

Realisation dawned. "You don't have a choice," Meredith said. "You're by no means stable enough to be sleeping on the floor. You'll just have to get over it."

"Meredith is right, honey." Beth rubbed her hand over Kathleen's thigh. "You look terrible and need proper rest."

Kathleen stared at Beth, noting the worry in her eyes. She would have to suck up her pride and do as she was told. Making Beth worry was the last thing she wanted. "Okay."

"Thank you. I'm going to go check on Chloe." After kissing Kathleen on the cheek, Beth followed Meredith down the hall.

Kathleen leaned her head back on the couch and closed her eyes for a moment, breathing deeply through the urge to vomit. She sensed someone watching her. She opened her eyes to see Stephanie leaning back against the fireplace, arms folded over her chest. This was the first time Kathleen had ever been alone with her, and she feared what Stephanie would say.

"How are you feeling?" Stephanie's gaze tracked over Kathleen's body.

"Like death."

"You're lucky you're not. Dead, I mean." Stephanie pushed off the fireplace and sat on the coffee table directly in front of Kathleen. "Meredith says she's forgiven you for the nasty things you said to her and the way you treated her. I believe she has, but I'm not so forgiving. What you did hurt her tremendously and made her feel worthless. After everything she went through, that was just cruel."

"I know. You're right." Kathleen didn't bother apologising. They both knew it would never be enough to erase the hurt she'd caused.

"You seem different from who you were a year ago, and I hope that doesn't change. From what Meredith has told me about Beth, she doesn't need to be hurt any more than she has been."

"I would never do that to her." Kathleen's chest constricted at the thought of ever hurting Beth. Several seconds of a slow burn passed, before Stephanie eased off on the stare, seemingly happy with what she saw in Kathleen's eyes.

"I don't wish you ill will, Kath. My goal is to make Meredith happy. But if you do anything like that to her again—"

"I won't, I promise."

"Good enough. Now, let's get you in bed so you can rest." She helped Kathleen stand and guided her toward the master bedroom. "I still think you're an idiot."

Kathleen laughed hard, which pained her arm. She found she didn't mind. It felt good to laugh. She climbed into the bed and settled under the covers. She tried to ignore the fact that Meredith and Stephanie had made love in this bed, and closed her eyes. A few minutes later she felt the duvet being lifted and the bed dip as Beth laid next to her on her left-hand side. Kathleen opened her eyes. Beth's were a few inches from her, red and puffy. Dark circles framed her eyelids. Kathleen knew she was barely holding on. She turned onto her side and gently stroked Beth's cheek. The bandage pulled tight over her wounds as she did so. She didn't care. Nothing would stop her from touching Beth at that moment.

"Are Chloe and Teegan okay?"

Beth nodded. "Both sound asleep. Meredith is going to take the day off work and keep Chloe occupied, while we rest for a few hours."

"Are you sure you don't mind waiting a few days before we leave?"

"To be perfectly honest? Yes, I mind. I want to be as far away from here as I can get. But I also want you and Teegan with us, if Teegan wants to come. And you're not well enough to travel right now. I don't want to be without you, so if that means staying here for a couple of days, we will. Darren won't know where we are. We should be safe for a while. But we do need to go, Kath, we don't have a choice."

"I know. He won't stop until he's caught. I hate what this is doing to you." She would give anything to take it all away. She wanted Beth and Chloe to be safe, to live a normal life, not to always be looking over their shoulders.

"The trustees will want to talk to me about the fire, but I don't think I can, not until this is over. If ever."

"Do you think they will rebuild? It would be a shame not to. This city needs that place."

"I don't know. With the investigation into the accounts and now this, they might deem it unfeasible." Tears slipped from Beth's eyes. "I can't believe he's done this."

Ignoring the agony in her arm, Kathleen pulled Beth into a hug and cradled her head against her chest as she cried. This whole situation was a mess. Kathleen just hoped Darren would be caught soon and they all could go on with their lives, together as a family.

†

Beth sipped her coffee then smiled across the table at Meredith, who mirrored her position on the opposite side. It was coming up to six in the evening and so far Kathleen had slept all day. Stephanie was in her studio with Teegan and Chloe, allowing Beth time to talk to Meredith.

"Are you sure this is a good idea?" Meredith asked.

Beth lifted a shoulder. "Darren isn't going to stop until he finds me. Everything he's done so far is his way of tormenting me. I don't want to wait around for him to hurt any of us."

"And Kath? Is this the right thing for her?"

Beth looked away. She couldn't answer for Kathleen, she only knew how she herself felt. She didn't want to do this alone. Having Kathleen by her side would make being away from her home bearable. But was it fair to drag Kathleen along with her? Beth looked back at Meredith, seeing only a genuine affection for Beth from her gaze. "She begged to come with me. I couldn't say no. When this is over, maybe we can come back."

Meredith reached over the table and grasped Beth's hand. "I hope so. We'll miss you both."

"Mum? I need to talk to you."

Beth glanced over her shoulder and saw Chloe standing under the archway to the living room. Her head hung low and her hands were stuffed into the pockets of her jeans.

"What is it, sweetie?" Chloe glanced at Meredith then back to the tiled floor. "Can you give us a minute?" Beth asked Meredith.

"Sure."

Meredith rose from the table then headed in the direction of Stephanie's studio. Beth held out her hand toward Chloe.

"Come, sit down." Chloe stepped forward, taking Beth's hand and sitting on the adjacent chair. "What's up?"

"This is all my fault."

"What is?"

"Dad."

Beth's forehead creased as her eyebrows pinched. "Honey, none of this is your fault. Your father is ill. He needs help." Beth didn't really believe Darren was ill. As far as she was concerned, he was evil. She lifted her hand and tucked Chloe's hair behind her ear where it had fallen across her face, then cupped her cheek. "No one is to blame but him."

"No. It's my fault." Chloe took a shuddering breath, her eyes tearing. "I couldn't understand why he hurt you. I wanted to know why. About two years ago I found some letters at home with the address of the prison. I wrote to him."

"What?" Beth tried to control her anger. She couldn't blame Chloe for wanting answers, but she may have inadvertently given Darren the information he needed to find them.

"I'm sorry. I gave him a friend's address so you wouldn't find out. I didn't know he would come after you again." Chloe covered her face as she cried. "I'm so sorry."

Beth stood from her chair and gathered Chloe in her arms. Chloe clung to her as she sobbed. "It's okay, honey. You weren't supposed to know." *That's why she looked so guilty when I told her about his release.* "Please don't worry about it."

"He never wrote back. I thought he didn't get the letter, so I never bothered after that."

Beth pulled back from Chloe, wiping her cheeks with her thumbs. "Chloe, it's okay. He probably would have found us eventually anyway."

"I know. I really am sorry."

"I love you, honey. Everything is going to be okay." Beth hugged her again just as her mobile rang on the kitchen table. She picked it up. *Brian.* "I need to get this. Go find Teegan." Chloe nodded then left, tears clinging to her lashes. "Hello?" Beth said into the phone.

"I'm ready to meet." Brian's voice was as she remembered, hard and roughened with age. He gave her the location and hung up.

Beth lowered the phone and blew out a long breath. *Time to go.*

CHAPTER TWENTY

Kathleen panicked. She didn't recognise her surroundings. The pain in her arm brought her back to the present. She remembered the fire and the hospital, and being at Meredith's. She judged it to be early evening, as the sun cast a dim glow over Meredith's and Stephanie's belongings. She had thought she would never again sleep in Meredith's bed, but there she was under the strangest of circumstances. Beth slipped into the room, closing the door with a soft click. She smiled when she saw Kathleen was awake and settled next to her on the mattress. She gently combed her fingers through Kathleen's tangled hair.

"What time is it?" Kathleen's voice came out in a cracked whisper.

"A little after seven. You slept most of the day away." Beth gazed at her for a moment. "How are you feeling?"

Kathleen took stock of her body. Her limbs felt heavy. If she took too deep a breath, her lungs burned. Her arm was tormenting her. "I'm okay."

"Liar." Beth grinned. Her hand made its way to Kathleen's cheek, then she lowered her head and softly kissed Kathleen on the lips. "Maggie is on her way over. She's going to take me to meet my contact. Meredith is coming as well. We'll stop and get some clean bandages and stuff for your arm and pick up pizza for dinner."

Kathleen's pulse spiked at the thought of Beth going outside without her. Darren had been relentless in his pursuit of her, and Kathleen couldn't shake the feeling she was going to lose Beth to him. "I don't want you to go."

"I know, honey, but I have to meet Brian. We need to have everything in place before we leave."

"How's Chloe?" Kathleen marvelled at the strength Chloe seemed to possess. *She obviously gets it from her mother.*

"We talked. She understands what's happening and why we need to leave. She's in the studio now, painting with Steph. She's worried about you."

"Do you think she knows about us?"

Beth didn't immediately answer. She stared at something above Kathleen's head. "She knows we're friends and that I care about you." One side of her mouth lifted in a half-smile. "We haven't really had time to talk, what with all the running from danger we've been doing."

"Maggie's here," Meredith called from the hallway.

"Okay," Beth replied. She glanced back at Kathleen. "We won't be long."

Kathleen didn't respond, too afraid she would beg her not to go. She knew she sounded needy, but the terror of losing Beth was ever-present in her mind and in her heart. "Be careful and listen to Maggie. She'll keep you safe."

"I will."

"Can you send Teegan in when you leave? I want to talk to her about what's happening."

"Of course." Beth leaned down and kissed her again, longer this time. Kathleen committed her taste to memory, just in case something bad happened, which it wouldn't.

Kathleen watched her leave and a few minutes later Teegan entered. Her head hung low, her hair obscuring her face. Her hands were shoved deep into her pockets.

"Teegan?" Teegan glanced up, her eyes filled with worry. "We need to talk." Kathleen grunted and groaned, as she sat upright in the bed. Her breathing laboured with the effort, and she took a moment for the pain in her arm to subside. Once the roaring in her head settled, she held out her left hand for Teegan to take. She did, then sat in the same place Beth had a moment ago. "I wanted to thank you for saving my life." Teegan blushed at her praise but didn't say anything. "You did a very brave thing, going back in there and finding me."

"It was a dumb thing to do," Teegan mumbled.

"Yeah, it was, but also very heroic. Thank you."

"Welcome."

Kathleen smiled. For such a strong, brave, young woman, Teegan embarrassed easily. Kathleen's smile faded at what she had to talk about next. Going on the run. Who would have thought her perfectly well-ordered life would have come to this? She had earned stupid amounts of money wining and dining the upper echelons of the finance world.

She'd had a lover she was happy with. All that changed in one night, when Meredith was taken and held captive for months. The last year had been a downward spiral to despair, and it took meeting Beth to finally feel like she had found her place back among the living. Darren's reappearance blew that hope away like a wisp of smoke. Their lives were in the hands of a psycho, and Kathleen knew she had to be the one to lead them all to safety. She wouldn't let Beth face this monster alone. Kathleen would be there every inch of the way, protecting her, loving her.

"I assume Beth has told you of her plans to leave?"

Teegan nodded. "Yeah. Maggie is taking her to get the new identities for her and Chloe."

"Did she tell you I'm going with them?" Again, Teegan nodded. "Has she asked if you want to come with us?" Teegan's stunned expression clued her in. No, Beth hadn't asked. "I know we haven't really gotten to know each other. You just moved in. The last few days weren't what I had planned for you settling into your new home.

"Teegan, I think you're an amazing young woman. Chloe loves you, and so does Beth. If you think you would want to come with us, we would be delighted. If you think it would be too risky and you want to stay here, I can afford to get you a place, anywhere you like."

"Could I have the mansion?" Teegan's eyes shimmered with mischief.

"It's hardly a mansion, but yeah, if you want it you can have it."

Teegan's eyes dimmed. "Does that mean you don't know if you're ever coming back?"

"One day, we might. But until Darren is back in prison, it isn't safe. As you said, even then, Beth might still be in danger from him."

Teegan stood from the bed, hands on her hips. "This all sucks."

"I know."

"If you're leaving, I'm coming too. I've got nothing to stay here for."

"Are you sure?" Kathleen didn't want her making any rash decisions. A life in hiding wasn't something anyone should have to deal with. Beth and Chloe had no choice, but Teegan did. Kathleen wouldn't put her in harm's way if she could help it.

"I'm coming. We're family now, all of us."

†

"Thanks again, Maggie, for giving me a lift," Beth said as they drove through the centre of town and toward the docks. It was eight at night, and plenty of people still milled about, no one aware of the anxiety worming its way into Beth's body. She trusted Brian, but he was still an unsavoury guy. Upstanding members of the community didn't go about securing fake IDs and credit cards for people. Brian wasn't somebody Beth wanted to deal with again, and if Darren hadn't resurfaced, she wouldn't have. The sooner she met with him, the faster she could get back to Chloe and Kathleen. Beth had left the hospital room believing she would never see Kathleen again. Seeing her outside looking desperate and afraid had shocked and worried Beth. Kathleen's plea to be allowed to come with her had thrown Beth. She was immensely pleased Kathleen wanted to be

185

with her, but Beth still wasn't sure leaving the hospital was a wise idea. Kathleen looked awful. A very pale face held dull eyes smudged with dark circles. Beth had yet to look at her arm. She knew, beneath the bandages, the skin would be blistered and weeping. Beth wondered how Kathleen would cope with her own scars given her aversion to both Meredith's and Beth's.

"Again, no problem," Maggie replied to Beth's thanks. She pulled into an empty parking space behind an old boatyard and cut the engine. "This is it."

Beth glanced around at the darkened area. The lack of streets lights added to the eerie feeling that settled over her. Meredith squeezed her hand.

"You don't need to do this," Meredith said.

Beth glanced at her and then out the window, catching movement from the side of a building. A shadowy figure emerged, wearing a dark hoodie and jeans. She looked back at Meredith. "It's too late now, he's here." With another squeeze of Meredith's hand, Beth opened the door and stepped out. Beth heard Maggie exit the vehicle, but she stayed back as Beth walked toward Brian.

As Beth drew closer, something about him didn't seem right. Granted, it had been a few years since she last saw him, but she didn't think he would have shrunk eight inches in that time.

Before she could turn and run, Darren lunged and grabbed her around the waist. He thumped her head with something hard. Her vision swam, but she could still see Darren raise his arm and point a gun at Maggie. He fired once, dropping Maggie with one hit. Beth screamed.

"We're going for a little ride, my darling," he sneered.

He dragged her to Maggie's car and opened the back door. Meredith lunged at him. The shock of finding someone else in the vehicle threw him for a second. He smacked Meredith across the face with the gun, then pointed it at Beth's head.

"You make one move and I'll blow her head off." Beth could see Meredith tremble as she leaned half out of the car. "Get in the driver's seat, you can be my driver while I keep an eye on this bitch."

With a gaze full of intent, Beth tried to will Meredith to run. Meredith shook her head, following Darren's instructions instead. She got into the front seat, and Darren pushed Beth into the back. He climbed in behind her and slammed the door.

"Drive," he demanded.

"What about my friend?" Beth asked.

"Drive."

Meredith caught Beth's gaze in the rear view mirror, her fear mirroring her own. She started the car and drove away.

"Get onto the motorway and head toward Wales," he said to Meredith. "Me and my darling need to have a little chat." After a few minutes of silence, he turned to Beth. "Where is Zoe?"

"Somewhere you'll never find her." That earned her another slap in the face, her lip splitting from the force of the blow.

"Try again."

Beth's head pounded, as blood rushed through her ears. It was all over now. *I'm going to die tonight, but I'll never let him have Chloe.* Beth resigned herself to her fate. She glanced up to the rear view mirror again. "I'm sorry, Mere," she whispered.

187

"It's okay."

"Shut up, bitch, and keep driving." He grabbed Beth by her throat, squeezing firmly. "If you don't get me my daughter, I'll put a bullet in your friend's head as soon as I'm done with her."

"She's with a friend," Beth choked out.

Darren released his hold and sat back into his seat. "Okay. Once we get where we're going, you're going to call your friend and arrange to have Zoe brought to me. You do this, and I might let you and your friend here live."

That was a lie. Darren was a crazy psycho. No way would he let any of them go. Beth just hoped that Kathleen would go to the police and wouldn't try and do anything stupid.

"What did you do to Brian?" Beth asked.

"Who? Oh, the guy you were meeting." Darren laughed. "You know you should never trust a criminal." He pushed the gun into Beth's ribs, causing her to cry out. "Seems he's fallen on hard times and faking documents isn't what it once was. He came to me in prison. Offered me a deal. He'd give me your location for a price. I would have found you myself, but I must admit, it did save me a lot of trouble."

Beth couldn't believe she had been betrayed by Brian. Darren was right, you couldn't trust a criminal. "So, you knew where I was even before I contacted him again?"

"Honey, I knew where you were the moment you moved."

"But why did he arrange to meet me? You could have gotten to me at any time."

"I asked him to. It's more fun this way. Besides, you were always with that fucking woman and then a fucking security guard. Mind you, didn't take much to put her on her ass." He laughed hysterically.

"What about Chloe's letter?" Beth needed to know if he had received it. If he hadn't, it would absolve Chloe of any guilt she felt over this whole situation.

"Her name is Zoe!" He jabbed her again with the gun. "My sweet angel." He sounded almost wistful. "Yeah, I got her letter. Brought tears to my eyes. How much she hated me for hurting you. I must admit, I did feel a tad guilty about her finding you. But she'll forgive me, once I tell her you're a fucking dyke."

Darren's hold on her tightened and in that moment, Beth knew how much he really did hate her. *Is it really that bad that I left him because I like women?* No, it wasn't because of that. It was because she was leaving *him*. It didn't matter why. Darren never would have stood being a jilted husband, no matter the circumstances.

"If you kill me, she'll never forgive you."

"We'll see." Beth could hear the smile in his voice.

This really is the end. I love you. She hoped Chloe and Kathleen could hear her silent prayer.

CHAPTER TWENTY-ONE

"They've been gone too long." Kathleen had been waiting on the couch for two hours. Her gut knew something was wrong. There was no word from Beth. They'd tried calling all three mobiles, but no one answered. Stephanie was pacing in a small circle, her fear just as palpable. "What are we going to do?"

The loud buzzer from the street entrance startled them. Stephanie went to the intercom.

"Yes?"

"It's Maggie." Stephanie released the door lock. Even through the grainy sound of the intercom, Kathleen could hear Maggie was in pain, and her fear tripled. Finally, Maggie called through the front door.

"Is Chloe in there?"

It was a strange question and one that threatened to drop Kathleen where she stood. For some reason, Maggie didn't want a thirteen-year-old to see her. That told Kathleen all she needed to know. Beth was in serious trouble. Kathleen went to the door. "She's in bed. It's just me and Steph in the lounge."

"Okay, you can open up," Maggie said.

Stephanie pulled the door open, and it was a good job she was standing where she was as Maggie stumbled forward into her arms. Her jeans were soaked through, and Kathleen gasped when she realised it was blood. Stephanie guided Maggie to the couch and helped her to lie down. Sweat covered Maggie's face and upper chest. Her breathing came in quick bursts. Kathleen knelt beside her, reaching her hand out to stroke Maggie's head.

"What happened?" Her voice trembled with panic.

"Darren ambushed us. He took Beth and Meredith. Shot me."

"Oh God," Stephanie whispered. "Not again."

Kathleen realised this was now Stephanie's worst fear come to light. Meredith had already been abducted once. She couldn't believe it had happened again. Kathleen didn't have time to think about that now. They needed to help Maggie, then devise a plan to get their partners back.

"Steph? Steph!"

Stephanie glared, her worry turning into anger that Kathleen knew was directed at her.

"Go find something to stop the bleeding. We need to sort this out." Stephanie didn't reply, but she headed off in the direction of the bathroom.

"It's okay, Maggie. We'll get you sorted, then you can tell us how you managed to lose Beth." She hoped a little off-colour humour would ease their stress.

"Sorry. Wasn't expecting him."

"Shush, I know. It's all right. You might be a badass, but even you can't stop bullets."

"Fuck, what happened?" Teegan barrelled toward Maggie and practically pushed Kathleen out of the way. Kathleen tried not to scream in pain when she knocked her arm onto the coffee table. Teegan grabbed Maggie's hand and kissed her forehead. "Baby, what have you gone and done now?"

Baby? Since when are these two that close? Kathleen didn't have time to ponder the question. Stephanie came back into the room carrying an outdated first-aid box. Between them, they stripped Maggie's jeans off and cleaned up the wound. To everyone's relief, the bullet had only grazed the thick muscle on the outside of her thigh and wasn't lodged in her skin. They closed the wound as best they could and wrapped a compress around her thigh, keeping firm pressure on the area until the bleeding stopped.

When all that was done, the four of them sat at the kitchen table while Maggie told them what had happened at the meet. Kathleen noticed Teegan didn't let go of Maggie's hand the whole time.

"What do we do now?" Stephanie's leg bounced with nervous energy.

"Obviously we need to call the police. We know he left in Maggie's car. That'll give them something to look—" Stephanie's mobile cut her off.

She snatched the phone up. "Hello?"

"It's Beth. I need to talk to Kathleen."

Stephanie passed the phone to Kathleen.

"Beth? Honey? Are you okay?"

"I'm fine. You need to listen to him, or he'll kill us." Beth's voice trailed off.

"I want my daughter." The angry male voice had to be Darren. "I'm going to text the address. You bring her. If I see one police officer, they die. If I see anything I don't like, they die. You bitches do anything stupid, they die. You are to drop Zoe off at the gates, then drive away. Once we're gone you can come and find these whores."

The call went dead. An incoming message beeped. The address was for a small village in Wales. Kathleen dropped the phone onto the table and relayed all that Darren had said.

"We should still call the police," Teegan said. "We can't just drop Chloe off for that monster to take."

"Of course we aren't doing that," Stephanie said. "Chloe stays here. But we can't call the police. He won't think twice about killing them."

"I'll go." Four sets of eyes turned to look at Chloe, who stood defiant in the archway between the kitchen and the living room. "If it means my mum will be safe, I'll go with him."

"Chloe, no," Kathleen said firmly. "We'll think of something, but you're not leaving here."

"I'm not much taller than Chloe," Teegan said. "What if I wear her clothes and go in her place? That might give you guys time to find Beth and Meredith, while Maggie takes out Darren."

Kathleen narrowed her eyes at her. "How stupid do you think he is? And this isn't some goddamn movie where we're all secret agents."

"Then what do you suggest?" Stephanie asked, her voice tinted with anger. "As far as I can see, he's going to kill them both anyway." Tears rolled down her cheeks, and Kathleen wanted to comfort her. She knew her touch wouldn't be welcomed. "We have to do something."

"I'll go," Chloe repeated. "He doesn't want to kill me. I'll go with him. Once Mum and her friend are safe, you can call the police and they can come find me."

"I have an idea." Maggie locked her gaze with Chloe's. "We take Chloe like he wants, but we don't let her out of the car until we see Beth and Meredith alive." She glanced at each of them. "I have an army mate, who is an excellent marksman. He can take Darren out."

Kathleen shoved up from the table. "You're all insane. He's going to kill them the first chance he gets."

"Kath," Stephanie said. "We don't have any other choice."

This wasn't going to work. Kathleen looked at each of them in turn, shaking her head. Darren was deranged. He wasn't going to let them live. It wouldn't surprise her if he killed Chloe too.

Maggie grunted as she rose from her chair. She stepped up to Kathleen and took her hand. "I promise you he won't miss. This is the only way."

Kathleen shook her head again, dismayed. They didn't have a choice. No way Darren would let them leave. Taking him out was the only option.

CHAPTER TWENTY-TWO

"I can't believe I'm locked in a basement for the second time in my life," Meredith said, as the heavy door slammed shut behind Darren. The two-hour drive had brought them to a remote farm. Darren forced them, at gunpoint, into the basement, where he then had Beth make the call to Kathleen. Just hearing her voice had briefly settled some of Beth's fear, before Darren snatched the phone back. Darren was going to kill them, then leave with Chloe. Beth had failed to keep them safe. She should have run the minute she found out he was freed from prison. If by some miracle they survived this, she would never forgive herself for putting them all in danger. Beth reached over and took Meredith's hand.

"I'm so sorry for this, Meredith."

"It's not your fault."

Beth didn't believe that for a second. "I wonder if Maggie is all right," she murmured.

"We have to believe she is. God, how could they let him out of prison?"

Beth didn't answer the rhetorical question. The basement door opened, and Darren walked down the steps carrying a fold-out chair in one hand and the gun in the other. He set the chair in front of them and slumped into it, a feral smirk stretching his lips. Beth despised him. She idly wondered if she and Meredith could rush and overpower him. Darren shook his head and tutted, pointing the gun at her as if reading her mind.

"Why are you doing this?" Beth asked.

"You stole my daughter."

"You tried to kill me," she seethed, her body vibrating with anger.

"Evidently, I didn't try hard enough. I won't be making that mistake again." His gaze shifted to Meredith. "I don't know who you are," he said. "But unfortunately, I can't let you go. You'd better make peace with God, because you'll be dying tonight."

Beth squeezed Meredith's hand tighter. Darren levelled the gun at Meredith's forehead and cocked the hammer. "No!" Beth's scream echoed off the stark, concrete walls. She shifted in front of Meredith as much as she could and stared down the barrel of his gun. "Please, please don't do this," she begged. "I'll do whatever you want, but please don't hurt her."

Darren grinned, uncocking the gun and pointing it into the air. "Anything?" He paused for a moment. "Well, it has been a long time since I had the pleasure of a woman in my bed. I suppose for old times' sake we could have a little fun."

196

He stood from the chair and grabbed Beth's bicep, yanking her to her feet. His intentions were clear. Meredith tried to hold onto Beth, but he was too strong and pulled her away. He pointed the gun at Meredith again. "If you so much as sneeze, I'll kill you both right now."

"It's okay, Meredith. I'll be fine." Beth didn't know who she was trying to convince. Darren backed up the stairs, dragging Beth with him with the gun still trained on Meredith. The sound of a motor reverberated through the room.

"That can't be her already," Darren said. "It's too soon." He pushed Beth back down the stairs. She stumbled and fell to the dusty floor, gravel sticking into her palms. "You make any noise, you die," he said, before locking the door.

Beth shuffled back to Meredith and held her close. The motor got louder and vibrated through the floor. Beth was sure it was the sound of a helicopter. She didn't know what was happening, but she prayed it was help. Muted shouts and thuds could be heard from the floor above them, then gunfire. Both women flinched at the noise. Another shot fired, then silence stretched an uncertain remission.

The basement door banged open. A bright light shone in their direction. Beth lifted her hand to shield her eyes.

"Stay down, stay down," came the command from someone, and the light moved to the floor. Beth saw four people dressed in tactical gear, all pointing high-powered guns at them. "All clear," the leader said into his radio. He knelt before them and took his face mask off.

"It's okay, he's dead."

Beth's sobs rang through the room, as Meredith pulled her close. "It's over," Beth muttered. "It's finally over." Meredith helped her stand, and together they followed the officers up the stairs and through the house. As they made their way to the front door, Beth saw Darren's lifeless body lying on the carpet. His head was turned toward her, eyes open. A large bullet hole bled from his neck. She turned her gaze away.

They were whisked into an awaiting ambulance, and after a quick check over, they were taken to the hospital. Beth leaned her head on Meredith's shoulder, holding her hand.

She was free.

†

Beth had been at the police station for over an hour. After she was examined at the hospital, the police took her to the station to give a statement. Beth had to relive everything, from the night Darren stabbed her through the stalking, the fire, and the break-ins. Finally, she relayed the details of the abduction. *Was it only a few hours ago?* She was tired and irritable. All she wanted was to go home. She still wasn't clear on how the police had found her, but she assumed Kathleen had called them. Meredith was in another part of the building, and Beth couldn't help but worry. This new trauma could set back her recovery. Beth glanced at the clock for the hundredth time, willing the officers to come and release her.

The door to the conference room opened. Kathleen stood over the threshold, her gaze immediately landing on Beth. Beth's hand flew to her mouth as she choked out a sob. In three quick strides, Kathleen was pulling her close and wrapping her arms around her.

"It's okay," Kathleen whispered, squeezing her tighter. "You're safe now."

Beth clung to her, not caring that she was probably hurting Kathleen's injured arm. Nothing would make her let go. "I'm so glad your here." She lifted her head, gazing into Kathleen's blue eyes. "I love you." Kathleen brushed her tears away with her thumb, then leaned in and kissed her hard. Beth gave herself over to the kiss, savouring the taste of her. She had nearly lost the chance to ever see Kathleen again. With Darren gone, she could finally move on with her life. She hoped that life would include Kathleen.

Kathleen inched back, her breath warming Beth's skin as she gasped heavily. "I love you so much. I'm so glad you're okay."

"Is Chloe safe?" Beth was desperate to see her daughter.

"Yes."

Keeping her hand in Kathleen's, Beth led them to the table, where they sat close to each other. "What happened?" She needed Kathleen to fill in the blanks of what went down.

Kathleen took a breath then explained, "Maggie made it back to Meredith's apartment. We treated her wound, and she told us what happened. Soon after, you rang. I was adamant on calling the police. There was no way I was taking Chloe anywhere near that prick."

"Thank you." Beth leaned over and kissed her on the cheek. Beth's biggest fear had been that Darren would take Chloe. If he had, Beth would not have survived the grief. Not that it would have mattered. He would have killed her first.

"Maggie said she knew a sharpshooter. Everyone was set to try and flush Darren out so this man could kill him." She took another deep breath. "I agreed to the plan, but before Maggie could make the call, I stopped her. As much as I wanted him dead for hurting you, I didn't think I would be able to live with the guilt, knowing our actions ended a man's life. There were also too many things that could go wrong, and I didn't want you or Chloe getting hurt." Kathleen reached up and cupped Beth's cheek, her eyes tearing. "I couldn't risk it, so I convinced them to call the police. We gave them the address, and they sent an armed response team out to find you. Waiting for news was the worst experience ever. I think I owe Meredith a new rug from the amount of pacing I did in the lounge." Her quick laugh became a sob, and Beth gathered her close.

"It's okay. We're all okay." They stayed pressed together for a few minutes. "Where are Chloe and Teegan?"

"They're fine, waiting back at Meredith's with Maggie. Once we knew you were safe, Steph drove us here. I think she broke every law trying to get here as fast as she could."

"We owe them big time for all their help, and for getting them in this mess."

"We'll figure something out."

The door opened again, and a detective strode in. "You can go home now, Ms. Jones. If we need any more information, we'll contact you."

"Thank you," Beth said. Kathleen stood and led them from the room. "Can we go back to your house?" she asked Kathleen.

"*Our* house," Kathleen corrected. "If you want it to be."

Beth didn't answer, she smiled widely and kissed Kathleen on the lips. "I think we should go collect our kids and go home."

"Stephanie is waiting for us at the front desk." Kathleen led them down a flight of stairs and to the main entrance. Stephanie stood leaning against the wall, Meredith wrapped tightly in her arms. Beth let go of Kathleen's hand and rushed over to them.

"Are you okay?" Beth asked.

Meredith lifted her head from under Stephanie's chin and smiled at her. "I am now we're all safe." She took a tremulous breath, her body shaking. "I really thought we were going to die."

Beth's guilt swamped her at Meredith's obvious pain at being abducted again. She stepped forward and hugged her. "I'm so sorry."

"It's not you're fault," Stephanie said. "You didn't make him do this."

Beth pulled away from Meredith and glanced at Stephanie. "Maybe not." She looked back at Meredith. "I just don't want this to set you back." Beth knew Meredith still struggled with her own abduction a year ago. Being taken again would be enough to set anyone back.

"I'll be okay." Meredith reached behind her and took Stephanie's hand. "We all will."

Beth hoped that was true. The detective had confirmed Darren's death at the scene and had put out a warrant for Brian's arrest. They didn't have much information on him, so chances of finding him were slim. Not that it mattered to Beth. She gazed at Kathleen. *I won't be needing anything from him, or anyone like him, again.* She planned on living a very long life with the woman she loved and their family.

CHAPTER TWENTY-THREE

Kathleen stretched out in her own bed, the early morning sun making its presence known through the blinds. She wouldn't be getting up anytime soon. They had arrived back home just an hour ago, all in need of much-desired sleep. Kathleen had showered first, while Beth spent time with Chloe before settling her in bed. Teegan had redressed Kathleen's arm after her shower, glad that she was able to wash off some of the ooze that wept from the blisters. No doubt, Beth would insist on a trip back to the hospital just to make sure it was all okay and not infected. Kathleen briefly closed her eyes, allowing her body to relax into the cool sheets. Her body had been tense for days, and it felt good to finally uncoil her muscles, knowing the danger was gone. The sound of the bedroom door clicking closed made her open her eyes. She watched, as Beth dropped her towel into the wash basket, affording Kathleen the delight of her naked skin. The scar on Beth's back registered only briefly. Beth slipped on a T-shirt and came over to the bed. Kathleen knew she'd been caught watching.

"Sorry if I woke you." Beth lifted the duvet and slipped in next to Kathleen.

"You didn't. I was waiting for you." She held open her arm in invitation, pleased when Beth snuggled in. Her head rested on Kathleen's shoulder and an arm wended around her waist. Kathleen kissed her temple. "Are the kids all right?"

"Yep. All tuckered out and sleeping like babies."

Beth's hand wormed its way under the hem of Kathleen's sleep shirt and rested on her abdomen, fingers drawing soft patterns around her belly button. Her touch made goose bumps rise on Kathleen's skin, spiking her arousal.

"How tired are you?" Kathleen whispered, squeezing her thighs together to help relieve some of the torment Beth's fingers were causing. Beth's only answer was to move her leg over Kathleen's thighs and straddle her waist. She leaned over, bracing her hands on either side of Kathleen's head. She dipped lower and caught Kathleen in a bruising kiss. Kathleen's hands gripped Beth's waist. Pain lanced up her arm, and she tried not to cry out. Beth must have sensed her discomfort, because she took the injured arm in her hand, moving it out to the side of them.

"If you want to continue, you'll have to keep this here. If you can't promise not to move it, we'll have to stop. I don't want you getting hurt."

"I'm already hurting," Kathleen grumbled.

Beth laughed and trailed her hand between them, stopping when she reached Kathleen's centre. The thin material of her sleep shorts offered little protection. Beth squeezed her hard, causing Kathleen to bite her lip from the pleasure.

"Promise me," Beth repeated and squeezed again.

"I promise not to move my arm."

"Good." Beth kissed her again and slipped her hand inside Kathleen's shorts. At the first brush of fingers against her hard clitoris, Kathleen nearly came. Thankfully, Beth moved lower, avoiding the most sensitive flesh, and sank her fingers inside. Kathleen groaned, pumping her hips in time to Beth's thrust.

They kept up to rhythm for a few minutes, Beth trailing kisses over Kathleen's neck and face before finally touching her thumb back onto her clit. The instant she did, Kathleen felt her walls tighten and her climax build. She let out a shuddering cry, gathering Beth and crushing them together. Not caring, she broke her promise and wrapped her injured arm securely around Beth. The pleasure of her orgasm far outweighed the agony of her blistered skin.

Her spasms slowly subsided, as she breathed into Beth's neck. The urge to cry filled her, but she kept the tears back. Never before had she experienced this kind of joy. For a few tense hours, she feared she had lost the only person to ever make her feel truly happy. Lying with Beth was the most glorious feeling in the world.

"Thank you," Kathleen murmured and kissed Beth. "Are you sure you've never been with a woman before?"

Beth blushed and shook her head. "No, you're the only one. That doesn't mean I haven't read a few things and imagined what I want to do to you."

"Oh yeah? Well, I'll be glad to follow your lead." She rolled on top of Beth and removed both their T-shirts. "But first, I want to show you how much I love you."

EPILOGUE

Kathleen leaned against the bar and smiled, as Meredith and Stephanie walked toward her. Meredith looked beautiful in her long, white-lace gown, her hair flowing around her shoulders. Stephanie cut an imposing figure in her black tux. The white flower pinned to her lapel set the ensemble off. Kathleen hugged Meredith once they reached her.

"You look amazing," she whispered into her ear.

"Thank you. And thank you for coming."

Kathleen turned her gaze to Stephanie and shook her hand. "You're one lucky woman, Steph." Stephanie glanced at Meredith, and the love that shone from her eyes wasn't hard to miss.

"I am." She pulled Meredith close but looked at Kathleen. "Have I mentioned recently that you're an idiot for letting her go?"

Kathleen laughed. "A time or two, yes, and you're right." She scanned the large room and spotted Beth sitting at a table with Chloe. "But hopefully my stupidity is waning."

Meredith followed her gaze. "I'm so happy for you, Kath. Beth is an amazing woman."

"Yes, she is."

"How is everything going between you? If you don't mind me asking."

"The last two months have been great. They have settled in well at the house and Chloe seems a lot steadier over everything with her dad." For a few weeks after his death, Chloe had been reserved. She'd slowly begun to open up. More than once, Kathleen had come home to find Chloe crying in Beth's arms. Eventually, the tears became less and less, and they lived each day to the fullest. "So far, Beth hasn't realised I'm an idiot and has stuck with me." She cut a glance to Stephanie, watching her laugh.

"You've changed, Kath," Meredith said. "Not that you were a horrible person before, but now you seem more comfortable within yourself. I'm glad you've found someone to fill your heart."

Kathleen was dismayed to feel tears gather in her eyes. She had spent months hating herself for all she put Meredith through and never thought she could forgive herself. Seeing nothing but care in Meredith's eyes finally laid that guilt to rest. They had both moved on, and she was pleased Meredith had found her happy ever after.

She had yet to contact her mother and try to make amends for the way she had ignored her father's beatings, but it was something she was determined to do in the new year. Kathleen had finally told Beth about all that had happened. Beth was sympathetic, but it had taken her a few days to fully process Kathleen's reticence to helping her mother. Even Kathleen didn't fully know why she had turned away. With Beth's help, she was hoping she could finally explore her childhood and find a way to forgive herself. Beth's compassion was the greatest gift of acceptance Kathleen had ever received.

"Thank you," she said to Meredith.

"Come on, Mrs Edwards." Stephanie took Meredith's hand. "We have some more people to say hello to."

Kathleen watched them wend their way through the crowd for a moment. She felt a hand snake around her waist. Turning her head, she saw Beth gazing at her with concern.

"I'm fine. Happy tears."

Beth reached up and wiped them away. "Good. That means I can tell you off."

"Whatever for?" Kathleen raised her eyebrows in surprise.

"I had a phone meeting with Margot this morning, about the fire and their plans to rebuild the centre."

"Oh?" she replied innocently. She had hoped Margot would have been discreet and not mention her donation to WHCC. Judging by Beth's mock glare, she hadn't been.

"Yes. She told me she couldn't wait to thank you in person for the five hundred thousand pounds you donated to the rebuild. When she didn't get a response from me, she realised I didn't know." Beth's other arm came around her waist, and by silent agreement they swayed to the slow song the DJ played. "You didn't need to do that. The investigation into the misappropriating of funds is over now. The accounts have been released. They could rebuild out of that."

Kathleen reached up and cupped her cheek. "I know, but I thought if I paid for the rebuild, the funds would be there to start running the centre as soon as you open. Saves you having to fundraise."

Beth leaned up and kissed her gently. "You're a remarkable woman." Kathleen couldn't help but blush. "Thank you for your generosity. Margot also wants to know if you'll stay on as the finance manager. I personally think she just wants unlimited access to your bank account." She grinned.

Kathleen laughed. "If she keeps sending you in to sweet talk me, she might have me broke within a month."

"The only sweet talking I'll be doing is getting you out of that dress when we get home." Beth kissed her again, then glanced around at the guests. "Have you seen Teegan? She promised Chloe she'd dance with her."

Kathleen looked around also. She found Teegan pressed against Maggie, grinding their hips together on the dance floor. It looked a little too raunchy for the song that was being played. "She's humping Maggie over there." Things between Maggie and Teegan had moved forward faster than Kathleen would have liked. Teegan was still only seventeen and just discovering her sexuality. Kathleen knew Maggie wouldn't hurt her, but that didn't stop her worrying.

Beth laughed at her disapproval. "Honey, they're young and in love. Welcome to the world of parenting. And don't forget, we still have it all to come with Chloe."

Kathleen groaned, causing Beth to laugh loudly. "I'm not sure I'm ready for that. Besides, we're in love, and we're not one step away from being hosed down." Beth nestled her leg between Kathleen's thigh as much as she could, considering they were both in dresses. She swayed her hips much the same way Teegan was doing, and Kathleen's pulse jumped.

"How about now?"

"You need to stop before I book us a room for the night, wedding reception or not."

Mercifully, Beth stopped, her body shaking with laughter. "Until home time then, sweetheart." She kissed her quickly on the lips and headed back to their table, where Chloe was chatting to some other kids.

Kathleen signalled the barman and ordered two more drinks for her and Beth. Her mind thought over the past few months. Who knew how fate worked and where it would lead you. Kathleen had been in such a dark place before Beth came into her life, and she knew Beth had been too. It had taken strange circumstances for them to meet and bring each other's hearts into the light, and it was in the light Kathleen wanted to stay, forever, with Beth.

The End

ABOUT THE AUTHOR

SAMANTHA HICKS

Samantha currently lives in the south west of England with her best buddy, Finley, her springer spaniel. She spends her time writing, drawing, and getting out into nature. Family and friends are the most important things to her, and she finds her inspiration for her stories from those closest to her. Writing has become her greatest passion, and after years of trying to find her confidence, she's finally decided to make a career out of it. She hopes to be doing this for the rest of her life. Sam has a thirst for reading, preferring it to almost anything, and she hopes, one day, to settle down by the beach.

OTHER AFFINITY BOOKS

<u>Wanted for Christmas</u> by JM Dragon
Belle Farrow knew what she wanted for Christmas–work. She had little to offer but a minor degree in cookery and household management. certainly not enough for a decent chef or housekeeper position. Then she saw an advert in the local newspaper. Wanted: Housekeeper/cook/nanny for the period of Christmas until the New Year. This is Christmas. Perhaps Santa reads the ad column too and pushes a little spirit of the season to that request.

<u>Dreams in a Jar</u> by JM Dragon
When you believe your life is a never-ending spiral of despair and the only personal joy you have is inside of a novel, would you grab a chance to hide away in the local bookstore and dream of adventures? Thea's life is about to embark on a journey she never envisioned when local bookstore owner, Marion, is taken ill. Her niece, Sheryl

Appleby, takes over the reins and her presence provides Thea the courage to take a leap of faith. Can she embrace the butterfly effect, or are Thea's dreams bottled in a jar forever?

Pleasure Workers by Annette Mori
Alex Cortez is accomplished at two things, fixing broken equipment and pleasuring women. She is happily doing both at the Ranch in Nevada. Danna Nichols, newly widowed, feels lost and alone. When her good friend Lindy invites her to check out the newly established Trophy Wives Club, it awakens dormant feelings and desires. An instant attraction happens and the two form a bond under unlikely circumstances. Will the challenges of their social status tear them apart before they can enjoy the pleasures of their new love?

The Trophy Wives Club by Ali Spooner
What happens when under-appreciated professional women are offered their dream jobs? When one of Atlanta's elite businesswomen and wife of a prominent judge sets her sights on a goal, life begins to change for these women. Friendships and romance bloom in a unique fitness club on the outskirts of Atlanta, where more than a workout is offered.

Unknown Forces by Samantha Hicks
Jennifer Wilson spent the last seventeen years raising her younger sister Kelsey after a boating accident killed their parents. Riley hasn't had an easy life either and her

friendship with Kelsey is the only thing steadfast in her life. When tragedy and secrets emerge, Jennifer and Riley must learn to lean on each other. The growing attraction between them only complicates matters. When events conspire to keep them apart, will they trust the unknown forces that keep pushing them together, or hide from their feelings forever?

A Window to Love by Annette Mori
Two life events, two paths colliding, two souls destined to meet. Mandie Carter lives an uninspired life. No passion, no romance, and just when she thought things couldn't get worse, life throws her a curve. Gail Forrester is barely hanging on. Buried under mountains of debt, only her much in demand architectural designs keep her afloat. Now, they must find a way forward together through what life and destiny has in store for them. Only then can they hope to step into that window to love.

Free Spirit by Erica Lawson
Priory McAllister has fought off boardroom sharks, handled high-pressure jobs, and thought she'd seen it all. She found her dream home and couldn't wait to move in. Unknown to Priory, two ghosts...Rhee and a mischievous Dylan...have inhabited the house since 1935. They have no intention of leaving. Jacey Ryder, Priory's long-suffering secretary, gets to play referee between her boss and a bossy ghost, as each side try to lay claim to the house. What can she do when an unstoppable force, (her boss) meets an immovable object, (the ghost) besides hope for a peaceful solution? They are like two peas in a pod—two *angry, stubborn* peas in a pod.

Addicted to You by Erin O'Reilly
Elin Prescot's dream to be a top fashion designer is finally within her reach—then Marissa Banks enters her life. Snared by her first taste of passion, Elin is consumed by desire for more. Her life spirals out of control until she meets Doctor Aimee Sullivan, who understands all too well what Elin is going through. Can Elin let Aimee into her heart? Or will her addiction keep her enthralled with Marissa? This story explores first love, intense passion, manipulation of emotions, and the gentleness of real love and true romance.

At Last by JM Dragon
A perfume company in trouble, leading to a town in peril. Old Loves. Unrequited Loves. New passions. Can the reclusive Gene Desrosiers save her family company and the people she cares for, even though some are not aware of it yet? Will an ultimate sacrifice win the day, or will Grady end up a ghost town of unfulfilled lives? This love story will warm your heart.

Deuce by Jen Silver
When Jay Reid was in her twenties, she had it all. A professional tennis career, Charlotte, the love of her life and a new baby. Charlotte's research vessel, *RV Caspian*, was lost at sea, leaving Jay to raise their child alone. Rescued by a local fisherman, with no memory of her life before, she lives on the Faroe Islands as Katrin Nielsen. Seeing a beached seal one day triggers her memory. Twenty-three years is a long time. Is the love they once shared strong

enough to be rekindled or have too many years passed eroding all hope of a happy ever after?

After Dark by Samantha Hicks
Can a love that starts out in terror be real or last? Meredith Ashcroft disappears on her way to a client meeting. Five months later, art gallery manager Stephanie Edwards is also held and tortured by the same sadistic man. Thrown together trying to overcome their shared ordeal, they find themselves falling in love. Is it true love or just an attachment to each other born out of fear for their lives?

The Book Witch by Annette Mori
What if someone had the power to bring characters from a book to life…should they be allowed to glimpse reality? Imara is that person, a book witch who is convinced of her superiority, especially over book magicians. Join award-winning author, Annette Mori, and the gang from Asset Management, The Organization, and the colorful women in The Book Addict to bring you this delightful, magical romance.

Calling Home by Jen Silver
Sarah Frost, director of the Frost Foundation makes her home at a writers' retreat—The Lodge on the Lake. Galen Thomas, who is taking a break from her vet's practice goes to the island to fill the post of handy person. A revelation of events from forty years earlier, threatens what they now call

home. Will the lives and loves of Sarah, Berry, and Galen survive the disturbing past legacy?

Reach of the Heron by Angela Koenig
After an automobile accident takes the lives of her parents and nearly her own, Arkadia O'Malley faces a painful recovery. She also seeks custody of her younger sister, Rini, and contends with Irish law. Arkadia's efforts to reunite with her sister are aided by powerful women from this reality as well as from Elsewhere. Will they find her in time to save her?

From Wind and Water by Laura Kovack
Surrounded by the Lands of Earth, Fire, Water and Wind is the Seventh Kingdom. All but Earth have rulers. A new enemy threatens all Lands and it is imperative to find the last ruler of Earth. Morgayne, ruler in Land of Water and Ventus, ruler of Land of Wind, form a tentative relationship in this quest. Will they allow or deny their feelings in this fantasy adventure?

The Book Addict by Annette Mori
This is a captivating story of Tanya, a young woman whose life is without any friends or lovers. When she meets Elle, the alluring owner of the new bookstore. Tanya is immediately infatuated with the mysterious woman. Maybe, the books won't be the only thing enchanted if Elle allows the magic of love to enter her heart.

Affinity
Rainbow Publications

eBooks, Print, Free eBooks

Visit our website for more publications available online.

www.affinityrainbowpublications.com

Published by Affinity Rainbow Publications
A Division of Affinity eBook Press NZ LTD
Canterbury, New Zealand

Registered Company 2517228